Praise for We've Already Gone Too Far

"This is chessboard horror. MJ Mars has arranged each story, each piece, into its proper place with sinister precision, daring the reader to make the first move. Narratively, she's always three steps ahead of you, waiting to unearth fears you didn't know you had. From urban legends to aliens, cryptids to curses, this author wants to play a game, if you're up for it." - **Nick Roberts, author of Mean Spirited and The Exorcist's House.**

"After a stellar debut, Mars shows she can sink her teeth into you regardless of the setting with We've Already Gone Too Far. I had a blast with this collection, and you will too!" - **John Durgin, author of Kosa and The Cursed Among Us.**

"If you like creatures of all sorts, this is the collection for you! I can't get enough of even loosely "themed"

ParaMonster Press

WE'VE ALREADY GONE TOO FAR

8 Little Nasty Tales by

MJ MARS

single-author collections, and I am a huge fan of cryptids, monsters, and creatures so this scratched an itch I've had for a long time. MJ's quirkiness and unusual combination of settings and plot details are both charming and absolutely brilliant. She has a sharp and ingenious sense of humor that most people couldn't execute in such terrifying, violent, and creepy works. She is so incredibly talented. If you have been waiting around to check out her longer work, give this collection a go for just a taste of what she is capable of."
- Megan Stockton, author of Lovely, Dark & Deep and Bluejay.

"A wildly imaginative - and often very cruel - collection of dark fiction that's well worth the price of admission."
- Duncan Ralston, author of Woom and the Ghostland Trilogy.

"After devouring The Suffering in practically one sitting I waited eagerly to see what else MJ had up her sleeve. Her debut was fantastic, hinting at top-tier storytelling ability and a wealth of imagination. I couldn't help but wonder what she'd bring us next. We've Already Gone Too Far shattered those lofty expectations with the very first story, and maintained that caliber up to the last page. Whether your bag is creepy legends, unique cryptids, psychological dread, or full-on horrific violence, this collection has you covered. An easy five stars." **- Ben Young, author of Stuck and Home.**

"This is one of the most ranged collections I can remember, and MJ Mars boldly solidifies her place in horror with eight stories that span the horror gamut. The end result is a collection that can only be described as batshit crazy in the absolute best possible way. Highly recommended!" - **Blaine Daigle, author of A Dark and Endless Sea and A Dark Roux.**

"MJ Mars seamlessly blends her unique sense of humour with innovative (and unusual) storylines to create horror shorts that stick in your mind long after you've finished reading. The attention to detail and level of thought that has gone into each of these stories is astounding. Every single story is high quality - there are no fluff or filler stories to pad out the book. I would love to see what the hell is going on inside MJ's brain because I would love to know how somebody can take storylines that have the potential to be pure cheese and make them genuinely scary." - **Sarah Jules, author of You Invited it In and Don't Lie.**

"MJ crafted a short collection that really blew my mind. Every story felt entirely different than the next. Each one finished just when I was wanting more. I really would read a full length novel or novella based on some of them alone. MJ was able to weave different styles of writing and it really showed me how amazing of an author she is. I am actually gonna steal the first short story and pass it off as a "campfire story" or a "local legend" next time I take my kids camping and they ask for a ghost story. This book gave me haemorrhoids, but in the best way!" - **Mike Salt, author of This All Ends Horribly and The Linkville Horror Series.**

"Eight nasty little tales that cover the horror spectrum, from bigfoot to big twists, airplane aliens to wild west weirdness. Ever wondered what a Wisconsin Blowdryer is? Wonder no more, because MJ will teach you! And believe me when I tell you that you'll NEVER feel alone in the woods again once you hear the legend of Jeff Among the Trees. You do not want to miss this collection." **Leigh Kenny, author of Cursed and Hush, My Darling.**

"I've only read the first story of this so far, but let me tell you, it scared the shit out of me. Jeff Through the Trees more than delivers. The building dread in that forest is just fantastic. And then when shit goes down, my heart was pounding." - **Ben Farthing, author of the I Found Horror series.**

"We've Already Gone Too Far showcases MJ Mars' true range both in premise and character, offering great thrills and a huge imagination along the way. Mars pivots from a classic urban legend, to claustrophobic horror on a plane, to gold-rush Western, Bigfoot, and the mysteries of life and death, each time with a deft hand and unexpected endings." - **Andrew Najberg, author of Gollitok and The Mobius Door.**

"MJ Mars' stories are so twisted, they'll make you cancel your next camping trip, delete your dating apps, and never look in the mirror again." - **Steven Pajak, author of The Haunting of Elena Vera and The Devil's Doorway.**

"Ever think women can't write horror? If so, you've been led down the wrong path. MJ Mars writes stories that will make you sit a while and think, do you really want to go on?" - **Danielle DeVor, author of The Marker Chronicles.**

"MJ Mars' latest offering burrows under your skin and leaves the reader with a lingering sense of dread long after the last page is turned. Exactly what this horror lover needed! I can't recommend this book enough!" - **Patrick McNulty, author of The Monsters & Mayhem Collection.**

"I absolutely loved it. Really well done. Every story is brilliant and unique but Jeff Through The Trees - for whatever reason that really fucking freaked me out." - **Tom Carter, author of The Doctor Will See You Now.**

"I read this book in the woods. At night. I still haven't recovered. It's so scary!" - **Angel Van Atta, author of In the Tall Trees and In the Tall World.**

"MJ Mars weaves fantastically dark tales in this gripping and frightful collection. This is a must read!" - **Jay Bower, author of Cadaverous and The Terror of Willow Falls.**

For my mum, Janice, who
"Doesn't love horror, but loves MJ Mars."

"If I was damned of body and soul, I know whose prayers would make me whole. Mother o' mine, O mother 'o mine" – Rudyard Kipling

"It's a funny thing about mothers...Even when their own child is the most disgusting little blister you could ever imagine, they still think he or she is wonderful."
– Roald Dahl

Note to the Reader

For Trigger Warnings and further dedications, please check the back pages of this book. Please note, the spellings you will find within these pages are the UK spellings rather than US. If you're a US reader, you will find "U's" where you least expect them, and "S's" where you usually find Z's. These are not typos - MJ is just British.

Thank you for checking out my book!

Jeff Through the Trees

Cora watches me rifling through the camping gear spread out on the kitchen floor, an amused look on her face. "You know we live right here. And the woods are right there."

I zip up my rucksack and stand, my mental inventory complete. Because she points toward the window my eyes instinctively follow, taking in the wall of beech trees on the edge of our property. "Your point being?"

"My point is we have nice, cosy beds upstairs. We have a TV. Tonight, while I'm enjoying a pinot in a bubble bath and watching movies, you'll be lying on rocks and twigs, less than a hundred feet away."

"We won't be quite that close, Cora." I plan to drive down the South track and park up, then hike toward the basin. Once we set up camp, I'll teach my son everything I learned at his age. "Camping skills are a dying art. I want Robbie to know how to look after himself if he ever finds himself stranded. Everyone should know the basics."

Looking even more amused, my wife says, "Be sure to watch out for Jeff!"

She cackles. It's a mean laugh, although I know she didn't intend it to be. Cora has a frat-boy sense of humour, which makes for plenty of fun over beers. But, when I'm trying to get something done, something important only to me, I sometimes wish she'd take life more seriously.

Robbie wanders into the kitchen before I can retort, both hands clutching the straps of his rucksack. He eyes the tent roll and supplies, looking uncharacteristically meek.

"You ready, buddy?" I ask, suddenly unsure of why I'm making him do this. It dawns on me that I haven't asked if Robbie wants to learn survival skills this weekend. He turned twelve six months ago, the week before my father died. For a moment, I question whether my desire to instil the knowledge that my dad forced onto me at his age is coming from a darker place than I'd intended.

Cora sweeps her arm around our son and grips him in a headlock, kissing the top of his head. "You look ready to me. All grown up!"

Robbie smiles, bashfully, and reaches down to pick up the nearest equipment bag. I'm proud he's taken the initiative to help without me having to ask. "I'm ready."

Sniffing the air, Cora holds up a palm. "You packed your deodorant?"

"Mom!" Robbie protests, squeezing his arms into his sides like a tin soldier.

"What? Just because you're camping doesn't mean I want you boys coming home stinking like skunks."

"I packed it, okay?"

"Reed?" she looks to me, the responsible one. There is a silent threat in her eyes. Not only do I need to bring Robbie home safe, but I also need to keep up with the hygiene rules she's been so desperate to enforce on our reluctant pre-teen.

"We're going to stay clean, Cora. Let's go!" I kiss my wife, trying not to feel hurt at the gleeful energy she exudes at the prospect of having us out from under her feet for a day and night.

We pack up the car and I set an old pop punk album playing through the speaker as we roll slowly down the driveway toward the woods.

The trunks of the beech whip past the window as we pick up speed, and I can't help but think of Jeff. I wish Cora hadn't mentioned the stupid local legend. It had plagued my teen years, instilling vague trauma every time my father took me out hiking and camping.

Jeff Through the Trees.

I snatch the air conditioning off, feeling ice cold at the thought. When I'd been a little younger than Robbie, my father had told me the story while we sat toasting marshmallows on twigs, the way they did in the movies. I wanted to immerse myself in things the grown-up teens did on my TV screen and begged him to tell me a spooky campfire story.

My father had popped a beer and leaned back in his lawn chair, eyeing me up.

"The scariest one you know!" I'd encouraged him, so intent on hearing a spook story that I had held my marshmallow too long in the fire. It turned into a blackened and bubbling blob on the end of my singed twig.

"You know what, Reed? The scariest stories are the true ones."

My heart had sunk a little. The truth seemed boring to me. I loved reading about monsters, watching Harryhausen movies and imagining what it might be like to face off against such wonderful and terrifying creatures.

Noticing my reticence, Dad pushed on with the story. "Whenever you come camping with me, I'm always keeping watch for Jeff."

"Jeff?" I'd parroted, my young voice shrill over the crackling fire. It was hardly a name that evoked terror, but something in my father's tone had me instantly on edge.

"Jeff Through the Trees."

My attention shifted to the treeline behind my dad, and, for a moment, I could have sworn I saw a figure pass through the gap around fifteen feet from where we'd camped. I sat up, adrenaline and excitement coursing. I was at that age where being afraid was a thrill that I would pay for later. In those dark moments of night when I wouldn't be able to help but obsess over the thing that had scared me. But it was worth it. It was always worth it.

"This story dates back more than a ways. Back when the land we're on was just one farm, owned by Les Highgrove. Les had a farmhand named Jeff, not a bright lad, but a hard worker. One day, Jeff went out hunting in the woods. He didn't come home. Old Les went out looking for him and found him stuck in a bear trap. Right away, Les knew the boy was in a bad way. Not because of the wound on his leg, although it was gruesome, alright.

Jeff was just *different*."

"Different how?" Reed had asked, leaning closer.

"Well, young Jeff had been one of those lads who liked to fill any silence with the sound of his own voice. Les had been used to tuning it out when they were working together, giving the occasional grunt when it sounded like a question had been asked. But once he'd got the kid out of the bear trap and splinted up his busted leg, the silence seemed like more of a chore than listening to the boy prattle. Jeff just stared ahead, smiling now and then, which was an odd choice for a boy with a broken and mangled leg. For another thing, when Les tried to help Jeff walk, he found that the limp was sporadic. It was as though he wasn't feeling any pain and was putting on a show for Les's benefit. Les was starting to feel more and more uneasy. Then came the kicker."

The evening sun had fallen low as Dad talked, and I couldn't help but notice that the light from the fire was dancing in the shadows of his face, just like in the movies. It was thrilling. "What was the kicker?" I'd asked.

"They came upon young Jeff's body."

In my mind's eye, I imagined the old farmer standing over the corpse, an imposter who looked just like Jeff standing with him, too close for comfort. "What did he do?"

"Just like that, the old timer knew that the Jeff that lay dead at his feet was the real one. He flung back an elbow and cracked the mimic on the nose, then ran back to the farm. He swore that the Jeff look-alike was pacing him, running through the woods beside him the whole way. Once he made it back, he called a group to go out and retrieve the body. He never went out alone into the woods ever again. And he swore that he saw Jeff most days, watching him in the trees."

With the fire crackling and the sounds of the cicadas chirping in the trees around us, I was suitably creeped out by my father's story. But it wasn't until he reached over and clasped my wrist that I felt truly afraid.

"Listen to me, Reed. If you ever lose sight of me out here and I come back different, you have to think of something to ask. Something just between you and I, that nobody else would know."

I think of how my dad once told me he'd called me Reed because he'd had a crush on the Invisible Woman in the old *Fantastic Four* comics (if I'd been a girl, he'd have called me Sue). But when I opened my mouth and started to tell him that's what I'd ask—the real reason why I got my name—he clamped a palm over my lips, hard enough to hurt, and looked over his shoulder at the trees behind as though he expected us to have guests.

"Shh, don't say it out loud," he hissed. "But always remember it. Just in case."

All night I'd lain rigid in my sleeping bag, too afraid to close my eyes. At one point, my dad got up to pee and I listened for every footstep. The stream of piss hitting the base of a tree a few yards from the tent. There were a few moments where I couldn't hear anything at all and when my father returned and re-zipped the tent flap, I squeezed my eyes shut and pretended to be asleep.

I wondered if the man lying beside me was really my dad.

And I never asked him for another campfire story.

Just as my weather app had predicted, it's the perfect afternoon for a lesson in camping. The sky is clear and the sun is high, casting hazy light over even the most canopied of the woodland. It's warm but not glaring, and our light fleeces are all we need to keep warm as we work.

I show Robbie how to find a flat square of land for the tent and oversee while he hunts for any rocks, twigs, or other lumps and bumps that might poke us through the canvas floor.

"This isn't *The Princess and the Pea*," I tell him when he holds up a tiny pellet of hard soil. I reach out and take it from him, then crumble it to dust between my thumb and finger. "I think we can cope with this. Let's put the tent up!"

I try to sound enthusiastic, but it is the part of the trip I always despise, second only to putting it away again. Robbie listens to my instructions, and his nimble fingers skillfully ease the rods through the canvas tunnels of the fly sheet. When the connections pop apart and get stuck deep in the material, he shows no sign of frustration or rage. He finds the snag and calmly fixes it. He's like his mother in that respect, and I admire them both for their patience.

When Robbie taps in the final guy rope, I test its tension and put my hands on my hips, admiring his work. "You've done a fine job there, Son!"

I get a flashback to the first time my father made me put up the tent, a year or two after he'd told me the campfire story. I could only remember snippets of time. Fumbling with the displaced rods through the material, frustration welling into tears that dropped onto the canvas as my father shouted at me to quit being a baby. Tripping over one of the secured guy ropes and bending the metal peg, earning a clip round the earhole. The lesson had ended with me sobbing by the river, my arms wrapped around my knees, wishing Jeff Through the Trees would come and swap with me.

Forcing the memory away, I pat my son on the shoulder. "Do you need a rest or are you ready for another lesson?"

Robbie shrugs, his energy boundless. The exertion has caused his body to expel a mixture of sweat and hormones but, unlike Cora, I don't mind. It takes me back to my own youth. The potent stink of locker rooms and sleepovers. Time spent far, far away from the woods.

For the rest of the afternoon, I carefully run Robbie through the basics of camping skills. We collect materials to build a fire and stack a ring of rocks around it so there's nowhere for it to burn but where we tell it. We go down to the river and I teach Robbie how to navigate. His eyes light up when he works out the direction of our camp on his own. We chat about keeping a clean footprint, leaving the woods exactly as we found them, and respecting the birds, animals, and insects. Robbie, always an empathetic boy, takes this on board without question.

When the sun starts to dip, I let Robbie lead us to the campsite and watch over him as he considers the materials we collected for the fire. I show him how to use the spark flint, and each time he tries to light the fire his hands are too slow or he fails to blow until it's too late and I try not to show the irritation on my face that my father did with me. My son catches my eye and looks embarrassed, and I feel ashamed. My dad's impatience every time I tried to learn forced me to do better. That's what he told me it would do. But now, looking at Robbie's defeated shoulders rounded over the flint, his arms reluctantly working to strike the light that might make me proud, I realise it was a hollow and pointless victory.

Switching tack, I tell him, "It took me years to be able to do this, don't worry!"

It's a lie—under my father's militant instruction, I wasn't allowed to go to bed until I'd perfected the art, the threat of his sulking disapproval worse than the prospect of a cold night with no heat source. With my fingernail hanging from the cuticle after I'd bashed it with the spark rock, the fire had eventually caught. Instead of congratulations, my father had sighed with relief and been sullen with me the rest of the night.

Now, I effortlessly start the fire, trying my best to show Robbie each step without making him feel like crap. I know he's tried his best today, just like I always did around my dad's strained encouragement.

Guilt is a gut punch.

His death is as raw as it was the day he dropped dead, and I am overwhelmed with shame at thinking something other than admiration for the man who raised me.

But still, it persists. A sense of injustice that it was so easy for me to give my son an out that I never had. It should have made me feel good. I should have liked the progress. But jealousy can stab unexpectedly, and even more shamefully, I resented Robbie for his easy life.

Unlike my dead dad *(fuck, he's really dead. How about that?)* I trust my son to complete some of the easiest camping tasks alone. I want to prove to myself that I am nothing like him. Before darkness falls, I ask Robbie to run and find more branches for the fire.

Robbie's eyes roll slowly, taking in the sky before returning to me. "It's not a cold night."

He's right, and again that sting of unfathomable irritation needles me. I always raised my kids to be allowed to talk back, and it's never been a problem. But out here, where I feel so close to my childhood, something else seems to take over.

I shake it away, with force.

"Sure, it is, Rob. You're right! But I want to teach you how to do all this stuff...Your friends will be impressed when you show them you can camp on your own. And you never know when a fire might come in handy dispersing predators." Robbie's expression mirrors my inner feeling of ineptitude. The older he gets the more frequent these moments of doubt hit me, rocking my sense of self.

My son slopes away, into the trees. I watch him stoop to collect a snapped branch. It's so easy for him. He doesn't even bend his legs and I want to kick him in the ass and send him tumbling down the hill. Worst of all, I think, he wouldn't even be hurt. Not really. Maybe a few scratches and bruises, but he'd be back playing with his friends the next day. If I fell down that hill, I'd break a bone. At worst a hip, at best an arm. The envy is real and suddenly I feel so mean I want to stick my hand in the fire to make amends.

There is a shriek.

It's a scream I know all too well from my son. It's the one he uses when Cora hides behind a doorframe and leaps out at him. It's the cry he utters at Hallowe'en when he walks past our newest porch jump-scare dummies. He's afraid. But only for a second.

I leap up and race to where I've just seen him. "Robbie?"

Time stands still. I guess that's a cliché. It doesn't. I hear the birds in the trees settling down for the night. I hear the cicadas begin their evening leg stretch.

Running forward, I imagine a vision of my son at the bottom of the hill, limbs mangled and twisted. *Why did I make him collect wood?* I ask myself. *There wasn't even any point. It's a warm night!*

I'm about to reach the edge of the ridge when the top of his head appears and he begins to haul himself wordlessly back onto my level.

Saying his name, I help pull him onto the path and hug him. He feels warm and rigid in my arms. "You okay, buddy?"

He nods, and I see the exhaustion in his eyes. Cora's right; I've dragged my son out here for me, not for him, and I feel like shit.

I guide him to our tent and open the zip, the interior doing nothing to ease my guilt. Why would I think that any child wanted to sleep here? In a stinking canvas dome with a cold, uncomfortable sleeping bag.

Without complaining, Robbie slips into his bedding on the right side of the tent and lays down.

"You sure you're okay, buddy?" I ask.

He nods, and I figure he's just mad at me. Mad that I brought him out here in the first place, failed to teach him *Tomb Raider* skills and still managed to injure him.

I briefly leave the tent to put out the fire. Then we lay together in silence.

I wake up with a jerk, remnants of a dream in which I'd taken a huge step off a curb lingering in my mind for a fleeting moment. I roll onto my side to face Robbie and blink, my eyes adjusting to the faint cast of moonlight behind the green canvas of the tent.

Robbie is sitting up in the dark.

He's bolt upright, but his head is turned away, as though he's listening to something in the woods. I can see his dark silhouette, his face obscured by shadow, but his ears protrude, giving me an idea of what I'm looking at. "Rob? Are you okay?"

He doesn't answer.

I grope around my sleeping bag and find my flashlight, thumbing on the switch.

The sudden burst of light illuminates the tent and reveals my son, staring right at me, rather than at the tent wall as I'd assumed. He is grinning. It's an unnatural smile that fails to reach his eyes, which stare wide and unblinking. He is motionless. It barely looks as though he's breathing.

He's sleepwalking, I rationalise, trying to ignore the creeping spiderwebs of dread that tickle my forearms. I sit up and touch a hand to his chest, trying to gently coerce him into lying down. "Go back to sleep, buddy."

The manic smile disappears from his lips, and an expression of belligerent annoyance shows for a moment. Then, he lays down slowly, with vampire-like rigor, and closes his eyes.

Unsettled, I shuffle back to lie in my sleeping bag but don't go back to sleep. Nor do I turn off the flashlight.

Of course, the Jeff Through the Trees legend begins toying with my brain, sending me flashes of abject and irrational fear. I wonder what question I could ask Robbie to prove that he is really my son and not a mimic, then flush with shame. I'm being pathetic, I know. And the fear of Jeff is nothing compared to the other thought that fights for the winning title of what might scare a grown man more in the middle of the woods; a dumb legend, or the idea that my son might have a concussion.

It had sounded like he'd fallen when he'd cried out, although he'd denied it. I'd thought it was pre-teen pride, but what if he genuinely couldn't remember? If he'd whacked his head on a branch and wiped out his short-term memory, we could be in real trouble.

I decide then and there that, as soon as it gets light, my son and I will pack up and head back home. That way I can keep a closer eye on him and get him help if he needs it. Guilt at bringing him camping in some strange effort to honour my asshole of a dead dad gnaws at my gut until I drift off into a light and dreamless sleep.

Robbie is already awake when I open my eyes the following morning. He's lying on his side, the sleeping bag cinched tight around his neck and plumped out around his shoulders so that he reminds me of the Shrunken Head Guy from Beetlejuice. He's just lying there, calmly waiting for me.

"You doing okay, buddy?" I ask, taking in his complexion and pupil size, and scanning for bumps or grazes around his hairline. He looks fine, but I know that head injuries can linger.

Nodding, Robbie rolls onto his back and stares at the ceiling.

"Well then, let's get packed up and head home," I say, trying to keep my voice light.

Robbie has this habit of recapping the previous day in the morning, especially when we've been out on an adventure or taken part in an activity out of the norm. I would have expected him to fill the tent with light chatter about the squirrels we saw or how the light shone on the brook as it skirted around the rocks, but Robbie is unnervingly silent.

When I assign him tasks; *"Can you pick up that peg bag?" "Make sure all of the embers are completely cold..." "Roll it tight, as tight as you can. Now hold it still while I try and get the bag over it..."* he follows my instructions without response.

Now, I'm worried.

My relief at reaching the car can't be understated. I had horrible visions of Robbie passing out along the trail. Of everything being too little, too late. I toss the tent roll and supplies into the trunk and get Robbie settled in the passenger seat. He sits ramrod straight, facing forward.

I turn the key in the engine and start the car.

Just as we move off, a figure bursts from the woods a couple of metres ahead of us. Robbie is covered in dirt and leaves, his clothes torn. There is a dark stain on the front of his pants where he's wet himself, and tears cleave tracks in the dirt on his face. He waves his arms, frantic.

I turn my head to the Robbie sitting next to me. He's still staring straight ahead, but the rictus grin has returned.

In sheer terror, I fumble for the car door and stumble out, tripping as I run to my son. I wrap him in my arms and turn back.

The other Robbie is now standing at the front of the car.

"Can you run?" I say to Robbie. He nods, gulping huge sobs.

We take off, my son just ahead of me so I can try and keep him safe. Looking back over my shoulder, the other Robbie is no longer by the car. I don't see him anywhere, but every so often I catch a glimpse of movement between the trunks a few metres to the side of us as we dash down the trail.

We make it home and I take Robbie straight to the bathroom. He lets me strip him out of his muddy red T-shirt and piss-stained pants and asks me to stay as he showers. He hasn't let me see him naked in years and I am flung back in time to him racing around the garden with no clothes on in the summer, Cora chasing him with the hose and pretending she's going to soak him when she catches him.

"What happened, Dad?" Robbie asks as I rub a towel through his hair. He's dressed in clean sweats and smells like the artificial citrus of shower gel.

"What do you remember?"

He tells me he tripped getting the twigs for the evening fire and couldn't find his way back to the tent. He roamed throughout the night, completely lost, but always hearing someone close by. "I called your name a few times. I thought it was you. But it wasn't. I don't think it was anything."

"What makes you say that, Son?"

"It was like an echo. I called for you, but the answer I got was my voice every time. It just said, 'Dad'."

He doesn't remember Jeff being in the car, nor does he question why we ran home instead of driving. It's a trauma response, I'm sure, but I explain to him that he fell and hit his head and so his dreams may have been confused. I tell him he was safely tucked up next to me in the tent the whole night.

I'm not sure if I'm saying that to comfort him or me.

When Cora gets home, Robbie runs into her arms and I find myself jerking forward to intervene.

Cora gives me a curious look. How do I tell her I'm frightened that the Robbie I brought home could be the wrong one? If it is the mimic and he suddenly tries to hurt my wife out of the blue, it will be my fault. And I would have left my real boy out in the woods. Guilt upon guilt. The never-ending cycle of parenthood.

I can't keep tabs on Robbie all day, every day. I dread a time when he leaves the house and comes back altogether different. Will I ever know it's really him? Or with every mood change caused by hormones, depression, or an inevitable switch in his personality that will take him from youth to adulthood, will I become less and less sure of whether he's still my son at all?

Instead of saying all of this, I explain quickly; my half-truth version of what really happened. "We got a little bump on the noggin."

Cora's face clouds. "Oh, *we* did, did we?"

I wither under her accusatory glare and then, while she carefully probes through Robbie's hair with motherly expertise, finding bumps without managing to hurt him, I look out the kitchen window.

Something red moves between the trunks, biding its time. It's a temporary reassurance that the Robbie standing sullenly behind me is *my* boy.

Amidst the canopy of the woods, I see the figure, waiting.

Jeff, through the trees.

In Bocca Al Lupo

Nobody could work out how Joe Donovan had managed to run the last fifty feet with his guts hanging out, the maroon mass cradled in his arms like a running back hustling for the drive, the snow in his wake speckled with cherry-blossom spatters of pink.

Polaris Squad stood at the hatch of the military compound, willing their comrade to make the last twenty feet to base.

"He's not gonna make it," Greg Marx grimaced, hunching over in sympathy.

"He's made it this far. Why not all the way?" Liz 'San' Diego snapped.

"Because of that," Greg answered grimly, pointing ahead.

It was difficult to see further than where Joe was slowing, his footsteps beginning to weave. This was due not only to the blinding sheets of ice and snow that covered the terrain, but the plumes of steam that billowed out from the waterfall. Polaris base had been purposefully constructed beside the Havasu Falls, built with ferocious heat lamps that kept the sub-zero temperature at bay. It was the camp's only source of running water, and while it couldn't exactly be referred to as 'fresh', having been recycled on a loop, it was as good as it got since the New Ice Age had struck earth. San squinted through the steam and saw vague movement in the distance. After a gurgling screech, the creature's hulking white shape burst into view.

"Run Joe!" Bunce yelled, hopping up and down a little on his tiptoes. He turned to Greg and raised his pale eyebrows, the expression lengthening his doughy face. "Why can't we go get him, boss?"

"Because you're an idiot," a few members of Polaris muttered. It was a stock-standard response to Bunce's questions, of which he asked many each day. A shrapnel incident during the Rime War of sixty-three had left the soldier with no short-term memory, and a long-term memory that ceased at age seven. Because of the team's now instinctive reply, Bunce rarely expanded his already limited knowledge.

"What the fuck are those things?" San breathed, shuddering. Yesterday's debriefing had been clear; she watched the photos and videos of the Ningen and should have known *exactly* what to expect. But seeing them on the screen just wasn't the same. She watched it gaining on Joe, a fifteen-foot white blob in the sauna-like haze.

The soldier almost came to a stop, his face twisted in hopeless agony. He must have been able to hear the creature gaining on him, felt the ice rumbling under his boots.

"Ah, fuck," Greg muttered. "He's a goner."

The beast loomed over Joe, standing almost three-times his size, its long neck craning up and over. Joe's head tilted back, exposing his angular Adam's apple, and the shock of the sight of the creature caused him to drop his guts. They unfurled, tumbling down the front of his grey and white issue khakis.

A gunshot rang out in San's ear, jolting her out of her stunned awe. Joe spun to the side and hit the snow, the trail of his guts hidden under his dead body, the bullet having passed through his left eye and out the back of his head, a dark splodge against his stark grey hair.

Commander Rale lowered her rifle as the creature turned its attention from Joe to the cluster of living prey waiting at the hatch. "Everybody in. Now!"

They slipped through the concealable entrance, one of only three that existed around the three-mile complex. Tucked away in the caverns opposite the falls, Polaris base wasn't the worst place San had ever been assigned to. The corridors were well-lit and spacious, and each soldier had their own modest quarters—a rare luxury. The heated falls provided a steady stream of water that was pumped to the wash-rooms and cafeteria, and each of the squad were allowed a three-minute shower and three small bottles of sanitised water each day. Compared to what she had in previous assignments, San felt as though she had finally made it.

The soldiers' footsteps pounded down the slanted metal floor, the squad subdued after facing the onslaught. This had been their first experience of the beast, their objective to lure it to the falls and try to kill it in the process. The briefing had suggested the task might be beyond all possibility, but San and the others had held out a quiet confidence that they would get the job done without any need of the falls. Now, they knew: their optimism was unfounded.

San followed Greg into the great hall and stood, waiting for the whole team to return. A distant clang echoed as the entrance hatch was closed and locked. San anxiously glanced at the four soldiers standing with her in the room. They waited.

Rale entered a moment later, moving to the wooden lectern, a futile gesture when there were so few people left to address. The previous day, there had been thirty soldiers sitting, listening to her instructions.

"Polaris. We've taken a severe and immeasurable hit today."

"Wait, Commander," Greg held up his palm, hesitantly. Nobody usually spoke when Rale was on the stand.

Surprising them all, she gave a small nod, allowing his question.

"Shouldn't you wait for the others to get in?"

Rale's eyes shot to the ground for a moment, her shoulders squaring as she composed herself to reply. Solemnly, her eyes skimmed the group before landing on Greg, "This is it, Sergeant. This is what's left of Polaris."

Yesterday
San sat at her desk and waited for the presentation

to begin. The screensaver on the huge cinema screen showed old photographs of the world Before. The sun rising over the Grand Canyon. A Hawaiian beach filled with bikini-clad revellers drinking cocktails from straws that poked out between brightly coloured umbrellas. A Dutch windmill in Autumn, the trees behind it bursting with leaves of red and gold.

San averted her gaze, staring down at her clasped hands and trying to dispel the wave of panic that had just hit her. She was usually fine. She could cope with the freezing cold and the barren landscape. She didn't mind the endless repetition of a life that consisted of keeping warm and surviving. But she had the kind of personality that always wanted what it couldn't have. And when she was shown images of women striding down sunlit streets in pretty dresses, or sinking into a bubble bath with an ice-cold glass of wine in their hands, she felt her loss as suddenly and savagely as if the New Ice Age had come yesterday, and not ten years prior to her birth. She consciously slowed her breathing, and gradually felt her heart settle into a regular beat.

Commander Janus Rale stepped up to the wooden podium and tapped the microphone. "You all hear me okay?"

The room mumbled the affirmative.

Rale nodded, then hunched over for a moment, her hands gripping the lectern as she gathered her thoughts. Eventually, she lifted her head, her red bobbed hair tumbling back into place. "Look, I know you're all wanting to know why you're here. You've heard talk of the creatures. Probably disbelieved the rumours. But I'm here to tell you that we are now facing a threat the like of which we hadn't seen prior to the New Ice Age. The altered climate brought with it something we could never have foreseen. The creatures only came to light eight days ago. They have spread far and fast. America is well and truly under attack. The recording that you are about to watch has come directly from the White House. It is an official issue. It is accurate. It may not be what any of you want to hear. But it's happening. And I need you all to pay attention."

At the woman's nod, the lights dimmed, and Rogers flicked the switch on the projector.

The screen filled with a standard confidentiality warning. It faded to black. A photograph appeared, from a long time Before. San could tell from the way the people in the image were dressed. Although, from their surroundings, they could just have easily been in the current ice age. They were flanked by glaciers, the ship moored in the snow, its hull coated with a crust of ice. The man at the head of the picture was looking proudly into the lens, his beard spattered with icicles, a stream of frozen snot making tunnels from his nostrils to his upper lip. He was gesturing with a gloved hand to two men behind him who were carrying a large crate towards the boat.

A voice over began, an English accent that enunciated each word with careful precision. "Antarctic, the year Nineteen Fifteen."

Cox spun in her chair and caught San's eye, knitting her eyebrows in confusion.

San shrugged a shoulder. "Watch and find out," she mouthed to her oldest friend, hoping she could see her well enough in the dim room. Lacey Cox was the only squad member wearing short sleeves, her skin somehow insulated against the freezing temperatures. She was renowned for wearing vests when the rest of Polaris swaddled themselves in padded foil parkas. She wore her long black hair in a plait, which swung back and forth as she turned her attention back to the screen.

"Explorer and archaeologist Duke Monroe headed a small team of twelve men at the behest of King George. Their mission: To find the elusive Ningen and return with a specimen for the London zoo."

Another black and white image flashed up on screen, this time showing a smudged pale blob against a black background.

"The team had already captured one adult Ningen on film the previous year, as you can see in this photograph."

There was a snort at the back of the room, followed by a few titters from other soldiers. San turned to see Joe Donovan covering his smirk with his hand and sinking lower in his chair so that Rale couldn't see him laughing. She understood being sceptical of the photo – it could have been anything. But Rale had told them this was no joke. She believed her.

"During their second mission, the adult Ningen remained in the freezing waters and did not engage onshore. Monroe found the creatures to be much larger than first anticipated, and almost conceded defeat, set to return home with their already secret mission a not entirely unexpected failure."

The image switched again.

"Imagine the team's surprise when they came across a cluster of egg-like pods in a nest at the base of one of the glacial mountains. Monroe was overjoyed. The mission was now deemed a success. They would take the eggs home to hatch at London zoo, who would then sell multiple Ningen to the highest bidders. King George would be thrilled."

The photo, black and white and with the same grainy smudges as the others, showed nothing more than a case of white balls. They could have been anything, San thought. But the slide changed to another, more recent image of the eggs. The photo had been taken Before, she noted, sunlight cutting through a window behind the box, the museum specimen room illuminated with natural light. The sight of the golden haze took her breath away.

"Unfortunately for Monroe, but luckily for humanity, the eggs remained static. No matter what techniques were attempted, science was unable to find a solution. Some even suggested foul play – that the eggs were nothing more than manipulated jellyfish. A Barnum inspired sideshow trick. The box was shipped from country to country at the turn of the twenty-first century, where science identified that the tissue belonged to a cryptid – a creature as yet unknown to science. But still, the eggs lay dormant. The box was eventually forgotten, dumped in a storage facility at The Museum of Natural History. But then the New Ice Age hit Earth."

The screen reverted to a crude cartoon, showing the cluster of eggs in warm temperatures in the year 2025. San watched the sketched thermometer dropping with the advancing ice age, the eggs enduring the gradually lowering climate until the 'magic temperature' hit. The eggs began to glow yellow. The creatures hatched.

The video flicked through a range of rapid CCTV clips, taken from the abandoned museum. Small white creatures the size of cats frolicked through the rotting exhibits. The cameras flicked from room to room, showing the white marshmallow-like bipeds growing as they destroyed cabinets and smashed trays of precious specimens housing samples of life Before. The final image captured one of the creatures in the Egytian exhibit, its face submerged in the bandaged dried jerky flesh of a mummy. It let out a screech and leapt through the window into the snow outside.

The voiceover spoke in an ominous tone. "The creatures rampaged far and wide, making monumental ground. Every ice settlement they came upon has been completely decimated. America's population has declined by 50 percent in the last week."

"Fifty?" Greg called out as the room erupted in gasps. "How can that be?"

"Eyes on the tape!" Rale barked.

More CCTV, this time the huge creatures traipsing up to campsites, tearing tents and the occupants to shreds before treading casually through the snow and ice, the terrain a perfect camouflage.

Bunce spoke up, "I still don't understand why it got so cold. I thought climate change was meant to make it all hot? How come it's so cold?"

"Because you're an idiot," Greg sighed through a roomful of hissed shushes.

San sat up in her chair when the footage grew more violent. The Ningen attacked the heavily fortified settlement at Chicago, tearing through the solar camp and ripping civilians to shreds. The snow melted into raspberry slush at the monsters' clawed feet.

The voice-over dropped an octave, and sombre music started to play over a still of one of the beasts at full height, standing and ripping a soldier in half. "We are in negotiations with Mexico to allow us to send our President and hopefully a number of civilians through the wall. As far as we can see at this time, Mexico is the only safe place."

Cox whipped round in her chair and grinned, her eyes alight with ironic mirth. San couldn't help but laugh at the irony, along with a number of the other soldiers in the room.

"Settle," Rale snapped.

Comments on the political movements of the past fifty years were strictly prohibited in the compounds. San knew better than to say anything out loud. But still, she took a little pleasure in the fact that the wall was keeping civilians in relative safety. And that those who had supported its construction were in imminent danger on the other side of its parameters.

San shuffled on her seat, trying to get the blood flowing to her numbed ass. On the screen, the picture displayed a fully grown Ningen. "The Ningen are fifteen to twenty feet tall. There were rumours that those that were originally seen in the Arctic were thirty feet. Perhaps given enough time, the hatchlings will also reach this height. But we do not intend to allow them to grow. It is no mistake that the US army has been placed at the sites of the largest artificial water systems in the country. The Ningen seem almost impervious to bullets. But heat appears to be their nemesis. You will now turn your attention to your commander for a full debriefing."

Rale re-took the stand. Hands shot up into the air around the room, but she ignored them. She rarely had time for anything other than her own agenda. "As you know, the water systems in the falls consist of gentle heaters that make the water just warm enough to prevent ice form. We have installed new, high-performance heaters powerful enough to boil the falls. Our mission is to draw the Ningen to the falls and watch it boil."

"How will the Ningen know to go to the water?" Cox asked in a clear voice, not bothering with her hand.

"Research has shown that bodies of falling water are the Ningen's chosen habitat. We do not yet know why, but we do intend to exploit the fact. The first step in this mission will be to draw the beast to the falls."

"But that's crazy – the falls are right next to the compound." Greg sputtered.

"Won't that be convenient for coming battles?" Rale gave the Sergeant a tight smile.

"Alright, that's enough information for one day. Tomorrow, we strike. In bocca al lupo!"At the good luck chant, the squad lifted punching fists and gave their bellowed response: "May the wolf die!"

Today

San woke up with the sick feeling of survivor guilt in her gut. She knew it well. The ice wars had raged on for years. But their dwindling population had faced nothing like this.

Just one Ningen had ripped through Polaris and almost eradicated them. Five left. It felt like a sick joke. And there was no chance of calling for cavalry. All soldiers were positioned at various bases across America, each squadron with one goal in mind: driving the Ningen in their area to bodies of rigged water and hoping that they boil.

Joe and the others hadn't lost their lives in vain the previous day, at least. Once the hatch to the compound had been closed, the Ningen paced the perimeter for twenty minutes before losing interest. Nobody was sure whether it would approach the water of its own accord. After all, those things were so new—so alien—surely any kind of scientific assumption was based on nothing more than a hunch. But the CCTV had picked up the creature slowly ambling to the falls, striding purposefully through the streaming water.

As far as they could tell, it was staying put. Just where they wanted it. A sitting duck.

San strolled into the canteen and balked at the unusual quiet. The remaining squad sat hunched over meagre plates, picking at their breakfast in sombre silence. She ladled a spoonful of eggs and grabbed a hunk of stale toast, then carried her tray over to where Cox and Greg sat opposite each other. They nodded as she slid into place beside Greg and poured a mug of tepid coffee.

"Too damn quiet, right?" he asked her, pushing his plate away.

Bunce leaned over from the table behind them. "You don't want that, boss?"

"Knock yourself out."

The private grinned and switched tables, pulling Greg's discarded tray towards him and devouring his leftovers. If there was one good thing about Bunce's lingering head injuries, it was his incapacity to dwell on the dire states they got themselves into. He was always cheerful, and although the squad acted like he was an irritant, he was considered by each with the fondness of a hapless younger sibling.

Cox sipped her coffee and leaned back, nudging San's shin with her toe. As usual, she was comfortable in just a T-shirt, her abnormally thick skin not even speckled with goose-flesh in the sub-zero temperatures. "How are you feeling about today?"

"Our chances?"

"Yeah. Yesterday was a disaster, but at least we got the fish in the barrel, right?"

"I guess."

Greg pulled the team's hand-held tech from his belt and tinkered with an electronic map of the falls. The heaters glowed yellow on screen. "It should work. I don't see why it wouldn't. Provided the water heats up quickly enough, there's no reason why we can't nail that sucker where he stands."

Cox grinned. "In bocca al lupo, right?"

"May the wolf die."

Bunce wiped his mouth and dropped his fork on the empty plate. "Hey, why do we say that about the wolf again?"

"Because you're an idiot," Greg and Cox chimed together.

Bunce let out a chuckle, never one to take heart at his allocated catchphrase. He sat up straight and raised his hand to his brow in a salute, and San turned to see Commander Rale stalk into the cafeteria.

"We move out in five, people. You'd better finish up. Those of you who haven't had a chance to eat yet—tough. Get your asses out to the entrance, or I'll throw you into the boiling falls myself."

San stood beside Greg and watched him key in the code to increase the voltage to the extra heaters. A warning popped up on the screen, and he swiped it away. Within moments, a rumbling sound cut through the drone of the falling water, and the still surface in the outer pool began to shimmy, bubbles pluming up from the depths.

Polaris erupted into whoops and cheers as the water began to boil, thick steam pouring out over the canyon.

From somewhere deep in the caves behind the sheet of tumbling water, something screamed.They snapped from their reverie and lifted their rifles, training them on the falls.

Rale pulled her binoculars from her belt and scanned the area. "Okay, team. We know the Ningen isn't gonna like this one bit. It's likely to come on the attack, but hopefully, the heat will have weakened it sufficiently enough to...hey, what the hell?"

The commander lowered her binoculars, no longer needing them as the vapour suddenly vanished, and the air switched to ice-cold once more. The bubbling water fell calm, and sheets of ice began to form in the shallow pools around the rocks.

Greg swore, checking the scanner. "The heater's generator lost power. It looks like it's blocked."

"So, what do we do now?" San asked, straining to listen for signs of the creature. Everything was quiet behind the gently tumbling falls.

"Someone's got to go in and unblock it," Greg said, grimly.

"That's insanity."

"No, he's right," Rale confirmed, in her no-nonsense tone. "It's the only way."

"We could think on it a little longer? There may be something else we could try?"

"There's no time. Getting the falls to boil is our one shot against these creatures. We are here to do a job, Sergeant Diego."

"Yes, Commander."

Rale turned to the remaining squadron and barked a stiff order to fall in line.

San joined her ever-thinning team, a squad that only the day before stood to attention in five rows of five, but now stood in one forlorn gang of four.

"The heater's generator had been compromised. Debris of some kind has blocked the line. I need one of you to go in there and remove the obstruction."

Bunce held his hand up. "I'll go."

Cox jabbed him in the ribs with her bare elbow and shook her head, tightly.

"What?" Bunce looked confused.

Rale wasted no time and strode forward, standing close to Bunce and peering into his eyes.

"Private, you understand that this is a dangerous mission. You need to enter the water. The Ningen will be very close to you. As soon as the pipe is unblocked, the water will begin to boil. Do you understand the implications of the mission you are undertaking?"

"Yes, Ma'am."

"Alright, Private Bunce. I am entrusting you with this task. I have every faith that you will succeed. For Polaris!"

"For Polaris!" the group echoed.

Greg moved from the line and clapped a hand on Bunce's shoulder, showing him the map.

"Okay, buddy. This is the blocked pipe. You need to enter the front left quadrant, swim ten feet, and make your way to Tunnel B. You got that?"

Bunce frowned, concentrating hard on the map. "I got it."

"Okay, I'll be here on the com, but you're gonna want to stay as quiet as you can or the Ningen will hear. If you get stuck, you can speak. But if not, stay quiet. Okay?"

"Okay, Greg. I got it."

"Good man."

Bunce gave the group a lopsided smile and raised a hand. "Okay, you guys. Wish me luck."

Polaris murmured their best wishes. Cox grinned, "In bocca al lupo..."

"May the wolf die!" the others chorused.

Bunce looked puzzled. "Hey, why do we even say that again?"

For once, the team remained silent, the usual insult forgotten. Greg nudged a fist into Bunce's chest. "Don't worry about it, buddy. You go get em, now."

"Oh. Okay," Bunce turned and began striding through the snow towards the falls.

Polaris kept their guns trained on their comrade, back-up in case of a sudden attack. They knew that their weapons were almost useless against their arctic foe but hoped their bullets might prove to be enough of a distraction to allow Bunce to run to safety should he need to.

San kept her sights on the falls, waiting for a looming white figure to appear behind the gushing water. Nothing moved but the torrent of warmed water.

Bunce approached the eastern bank and crouched, gingerly inching his booted foot into the lapping water. He glanced back at the troupe and grinned. Then he pushed himself off the embankment and slipped into the waist-high water.

Greg adjusted his headset, holding the digital map close, ready to instruct the hapless soldier should he get lost. With Bunce, there was a fine chance of that. Hell, San thought, he might forget what he's doing entirely and head in the wrong direction. She was glad of the trackers they all had fitted to their sternums, the faint fleck of blue on the screen telling Greg where Bunce would be at all times. "Glad you've got the tracker on him."

"It's a shame we can't get trackers into the damned Ningen," Greg muttered with a wry smile.

"Would make our lives a hell of a lot easier."

"Are you volunteering to undertake that task?" Rale asked, sharply.

"No, Ma'am."

"Didn't think so. And I also think that if you can't work out where a Ningen is without being shown on a screen, you've got a serious eyesight issue."

Greg dipped his head and suppressed a surprised laugh, his eyebrows flickering towards his hairline. The usually grim commander was uncharacteristically perky, the worst of situations bringing out the best of her humour. He opened his mouth to give a tentative reply when his mic gave a bursting fizz as Bunce breathed into the open line.

"Greg? Hey Greg..." Bunce spoke.

"Ssh! Don't forget to keep your voice down in there, buddy," Greg hissed.

"Right, right..." Bunce lowered his volume to a mumble, and San could hear the echoing sound of the soldier wading through the water, the steady churn of the falls behind him. "I just got to thinkin' I might be a little lost."

"No, you're doing good." Greg peered down at the monitor. "The pipe is straight up ahead. When you get to a hole in the side wall, that's where the heater is situated."

San huddled closer to Greg, listening intently as Bunce shuffled through the depths, his arms causing splashes as they cut the surface. "He really needs to cool it with the noise," she warned.

"I know." Greg nodded and lifted his mic, whispering, "Bunce, go slower through the water. Those splashes sound pretty loud. Remember, those assholes can hear."

The noises eased until the only sound was the static rumble of the falls echoing around the caverns. A few moments later, the blue light on the monitor reached the yellow dot that indicated the blocked heater. Bunce's voice sounded once more. "Okay, I'm at the entrance to the generator. I'm gonna reach in."

"Careful, now. We don't know what's in there, remember."

"I got my fingers on something...it feels like material."

"Material?" Rale queried, with a frown. "Why would there be material down there?"

"I'm gonna give it a tug."

The group listened to the sounds of Bunce yanking at the blockage, groaning with exertion.

"It's coming...I got it. It's AGH!"

Greg nearly dropped the monitor at Bunce's piercing cry. "Shit, what is it?"

"It's Joe! It's Donovan's chest with no arms or legs!"

Cox shook her head. "Get him out of there, Greg. If that thing didn't hear him scream, I'll eat my own fucking head."

"Get out of there, buddy! Water temp is rising."

"I know, I can feel it."

The group listened as Bunce began to swim, the choppy kicks of a bumbling front crawl.

"Remember to keep quiet..." Greg hissed.

"Negative, Sergeant!" Bunce cried, panting. "The enemy has me in its sights anyway."

"Oh, shit!" Cox hissed. "How far is he from the edge?"

"Just a click."

"Jesus..."

Bunce's voice came over the speaker. "Dang, Sarg, it's getting hotter than a whore's armpit down here."

"You're almost out, Bunce. Where is the Ningen?"

"I dunno. I think he's in the water with me. Ouch, my god, this water's startin' to sting!"

"The good news is that there's plenty of ice out here to help your burns, Private."

"Hah! I hear that! Okay, I'm almost out, I can see the edge." They listened as a burst of static cut through the com, followed by a muffled cry.

Greg's back grew stiff. "Bunce?"

The team craned their necks as a collective, as though straining to hear their comrade would make his voice magically appear down the coms line.

It didn't.

"Shit!" Cox blurted, kicking at the frozen ground.

They stared at the falls, the water now churning and bubbling, the great blanket of thick steam re-emerging and floating towards them.

Behind the tumult, an inhuman screech rang out. The Ningen.

Rale stepped forward, raising her pistol. "Okay, it's working. That was a scream of pain."

"Or anger," San mumbled, unease creeping through her system.

Rale lifted an arm, motioning for the team to stay put, and trotted forward a few paces. "I think I see something."

The mist was thickening, the water rumbling to fervent temperatures. San squinted, trying to visualise the falls as the sheet of white closed it off. Through the murk, a black speck became visible. It grew larger as it hurtled towards them.

Rale flew back three feet and landed sprawled on the ice, hit by a missile that had been thrown from the falls with inhuman force. The object pinned her to the ground. San realised with sudden sick clarity that it was Bunce's torso, limbs shorn away, his boiled skin blistering and pink all over, his hair hanging from a slack scalp and dripping into Rale's mouth.

Greg lurched forward and grabbed the corpse's shoulder, lifting it away from the commander. One of Bunce's eyes plopped from its shattered housing and draped over Rale's cheek, dangling from the optic nerve.

"Get it off me!" The usually stoic commander barked, and San dashed forward to help Greg. It wasn't that Bunce's chest was particularly heavy. It was just impossible to find enough purchase to grip, the bubbling skin slippery and blubberlike in their hands. Together, they wrestled the hunk of flesh to the side, and Rale clambered to her feet, visibly shaken.

Greg moved to comfort her and found himself on the receiving end of a sharp slap.

"Don't you dare touch me, Sergeant!" Rale bit, then whipped her head in the direction of the falls as the Ningen shrieked again.

San had heard that cry out on the field.

A battle cry.

A gentle gust of wind whipped eerily through the canyon, carrying the brunt of the mist with it and giving Polaris a sudden clear view of the waterfall.

The Ningen burst through the sheet of water and stood for a moment, the blistering stream coursing down its back. It clenched its hands at its sides, lifted its head, and roared, sending an avalanche of both real and artificial rock tumbling down around it. Snorting, it pitched forwards and began to race towards them.

"Hold your ground, Polaris!" Rale yelled.

San's hands quivered as she lifted her rifle, took aim, and fired at the Ningen's bulbous head. She aimed as best as she could towards what appeared to be the creature's eyes, but she couldn't be sure. It was like fighting a giant marshmallow.

The Ningen was pounding over the ground toward them, and suddenly the wind dropped, the cavern filling with mist once more and plunging the air into silence.

San heard nothing but her own rapid breathing, trailing her gun through the white. Even the muzzle of the gun was swept up in the steam. The fog stung her eyes. She blinked through tears and struggled to listen for the creature. With the fall of the sudden mist, the Ningen's pounding footsteps had halted.

"Where the fuck is it?" Greg cried.

Cox sent a burst of shots ringing into the white.

"You see it?"

"No, but it's worth a shot."

As one, the team began to fire in the direction of where the Ningen had been charging towards them. It made no sense that it had come to a stop before finishing its assault. "Why isn't it attacking?" San yelled.

Rale blasted her pistol into the ether. "I think it's as confused by the mist as we are."

San ceased fire and waited. For all they knew, their shots had done the trick, even if the boiling water hadn't.

Following her lead, the team lowered their weapons and waited, the mist curling around their faces and limbs and giving them a peculiar ghostly appearance. San didn't much care for that thought and tried to push it from her mind.

Cox looked over at her, her face almost obscured. "Do you think we killed it?"

The words were only just out of her mouth when a giant white fist sledgehammered down through the steam and smashed into the top of her head, pulverising her into the ice. The mist around her grew pink, and the splashback of her blood exploding through her bursting skin dappled San's face.

The wind gusted again, dissipating the steam, and San looked up to find the monster looming over them, gore from Cox's disintegrated body streaking its right arm. It screamed in delight at finding its prey and reached down to pluck Rale up in its fist.

Greg began to fire at the hand, but his bullets were like gnat bites.

Rale tried to raise her pistol, but the monster squeezed, and her spine snapped and crunched, the pistol slipping from her paralysed fingers and tumbling ten feet to the ground. The Ningen lifted her doll-like body to its face, opened its slit of a mouth, and bit off her head.

"God damnit!" Greg yelled, pulling out his machete and rushing to the creature's feet. He leapt into the air and drove the knife down, the blade disappearing into the strange luminescent flesh.Unperturbed, the Ningen tossed Rale's body to the side and spat her head from its mouth, launching it like a cannonball.

San dodged the tumbling head and ran around the side of the creature, scanning its body and looking for weakness. Catching a glimpse of its back, she blinked up and felt a flicker of hope before the mist once more closed in on the scene. Where the scalding falls had tumbled down the monster's back, the shimmering white flesh had turned a mottled grey, some of the skin hanging torn and singed, revealing pink inner flesh beneath. Their plan was good, after all. They had to get it back into the falls.

San wanted to yell out to Greg but needed to get into a better position before attracting the Ningen's attention. She pumped through the snow and ice, her feet sliding, losing traction in the sludge created by the heat from the newly boiling falls. She made her way through the steam, slowing when the noise from the water grew closer. The last thing she needed was to fall in and boil to death before she'd even got the Ningen to attack.

Once positioned at the side of the falls, San tugged a flare from her belt and set it blaring, tossing it at her feet. She could hear gunshots and the roar of the monster coming from the direction of the attack. She wished she could see what was going on and willed the wind to gust through the canyon once more.

All fell silent, except for the steady thrum of the bubbling falls to her right. The vapour billowed, growing thicker. She could feel it in the back of her throat when she breathed, and her eyes streamed hot liquid over her cheeks whenever she blinked. The flare burnt itself out. All remained quiet.

Everything was white. The white of the earth at her feet. The white of the steam and the white of the bleak, cloud-covered sky. The white of the Ningen. How ironic, she thought, that she had one foe in this battle, and it had become completely camouflaged by the very weapon they had chosen to use against it.

She waited, blinking in the mist.

As gently as she could, San reached for her second flare, then froze. She could have sworn she heard a grunting sound coming from the mist in front of her. She abandoned the flare and reached instead for her pistol, lifting it from its holster and holding it steady in front of her chest.

A shape loomed in front of her. Her finger fluttered over the trigger, ready. But the visage was dark and human-height, and as it inched closer, she could see that it was Greg.

"Jesus, man," she hissed, lowering the weapon. "You scared me half to death."

Through the vapour, Greg's head tilted to one side, dropping toward his shoulder.

"It's me...it's San." She strode forward.

Greg moved closer at the same time, his movements eerily smooth, and the steam parted around his features when he came near enough for San to reach out and touch him. His eyes were open, but the lids drooped at the edges. His mouth twisted down in an exaggerated sneer, and his skin had a blueish tinge. Still, he stepped forward. Or, more accurately, he glided. The tracking device dropped from his fingers and landed at her feet.

San gently pressed her palm into his chest, and his body rocked against her touch.

She blinked, taking in the peculiar tilt of his head, his unfocused stare, and the way his body swayed as though it was dangling from a thread, puppet-like.

A smooth white spike protruded from Greg's neck, a trickle of rapidly drying blood streaking down under his collar. Above San, the Ningen sniffed the air, disturbing the steam enough for her to make out its looming white shape. It had stuck its fingertip through Greg's neck, and was pushing him along. A lure.

San rolled backwards, dodging the strike just in time.

The Ningen lifted its hand to the side and swung it

back, Greg's body a pendulum in the space where she had just been standing.

San scrambled to her feet and grabbed the tracker, shoving it into her belt. She dashed towards the wall of rocks, hooking her fingers around the jutting handholds and hauling herself up the rock face. To her left, the bubbling falls steamed, splashes of scalding water dappling her clothing. She braced herself against the sudden shock of the burns against her skin and flung herself sideways, behind the flow of the falls.

It was like a sauna, the thundering noise of the tumbling water enveloping her senses, the hot steam scalding her lungs and sending droplets of sweat cascading from her pores. She heard the Ningen erupt into a scream of frustration at losing her. It was primed for attack. Now was her best chance at getting it to give chase.

San rested back into a crevasse, leaning hard into her backside and pressing her feet against the solid rock beneath her. She lifted the second flare from her belt and struck it, sparking it to life. She held it out in front of her, the red shine illuminating the water and making her feel as though she was sitting in an erupting volcano.

The Ningen burst through the falls, the red water tumbling down its shoulders. It stood for a moment under the torrent, its slit-like eyes screwed up hard against its smooth, marshmallow face. San raised her machine gun, holding off on using it. She didn't want to push the creature back out of the falls before it had sustained significant injury.

The monster seemed puzzled. It stood frozen under the scalding flow, watching her watching him. It let out a small screech, and white blubber-like flesh began to sluice from its shoulders, revealing pink matter below. It turned its head to peer at one of its stripped shoulders, and the stream caught its cheek. Its face eroded, white flesh tumbling into its neck.

It was working.

Seeing her chance, San trained the machine gun on the exposed pink under-flesh and shot a quick-fire round of bullets into its face.

The Ningen dropped to its knees, shaking the falls. Rocks scattered down the mountain face around her and San flung her elbow back into the crevasse to steady herself. Secured, she fired again, her bullets trailing over the sides of the monster where the water was coursing, tearing layer after layer of skin from its body. Chunks of pink matter exploded from the creature's diminished frame. It gave a bemused-sounding groan, pitched forward, and landed half-face first in the bubbling basin of the waterfall.

San waited a few moments, watching the scalding stream eat through its back, cutting the creature's body in two. Like a fatty chicken carcass dissolving in the stew pot, soon, all that remained of the Ningen were floating blobs of decimated and ragged white flesh. It was dead.

But at what cost? Her elation quickly dampened. The rest of Polaris had been wiped out.

San took the electronic tracker from her belt and typed in her code. Recalling the steps Greg had taught her in debriefing, she disabled the secondary heaters, ensuring the primary warmers were still engaged so that she would have fresh water in the complex while she waited for extraction.

She scrambled out from behind the falls and retreated down the rock face, dropping into the sludgy snow. The cessation of the heaters caused the steam to dissipate. It was hazy, but clear enough to get her general bearings. San set off striding towards the entrance to the mission base. She wiped sweat from her face with her sleeve and blinked a few times, adjusting to her surroundings now that the thick blanket of white was beginning to lift.

She was almost at the camp when she found the spatters of blood indicating where Cox had fallen. She stopped and gave a momentary thought to her friend. Rale lay a few metres away, her headless corpse twisted, limbs tangled and squeezed.

The hairs on San's neck bristled as she suddenly felt eyes on her, the heart-sinking sensation of being watched. She spun on her heels.

A second Ningen stepped out of the thinning mist, no more than two metres away from her. It let out a horrifying scream, a battle cry San recognised from the field.

Flexing its fingers, revealing five-inch talons as white as the ground at her feet, it stepped forward and swiped before San had time to think about lifting her gun. Not that it would have made much difference, she knew.

She saw her own chest rising up to meet her face, her view skimming all the way down the front of her torso and thighs as her head and shoulders pitched into an extreme forward bend. She would have touched her toes, but her arms hung loose, all signals to her brain severed at the spine.

Her face and shoulders landed in the snow, and for a few seconds, all she could see was white.

The 'Fasten Seatbelt' Light is On

The plane cruised over **Salt Lake City** and turbulence from the surrounding mountains sent a judder through the cabin. Miniature plastic wine bottles clunked together on the trolley, and ice made scratching sounds in its cooler tray.

Rhea made eye contact with the little girl, Dot, who was travelling alone. Dot peered over the top of her Nintendo Switch at the first hint of movement and Rhea smiled, willing the girl to remember what she'd told her; "If you get scared, look at the flight attendants. If we're not worried, you don't have to be."

The kid pressed her lips together and gave a small nod before returning to her game. Dot was an apt name for her. Swamped by oversized cargo shorts and a dance studio sweater, she had the coltish knees and elbows of a girl who would be tiny of stature into adulthood. Her hair was cut into a wispy pixie cut that emphasised her almond eyes and small mouth, the heart-shaped face adding to her elfin appearance. As she played her game, her hands leapt each time her character jumped, and she leaned slightly in the direction she wanted to turn, so immersed in play she didn't notice that her body was at one with the pixels on the screen. It was meeting kids like this and knowing she would have a positive impact on their flight experience that made all the crap that came with Rhea's job worthwhile.

Becoming a cabin crew member had been one of the most important moments of Rhea's life. She'd been a sheltered girl, not because of her upbringing, but because of something inside her that wouldn't allow her to settle without a looming sense of fear. She'd lived her early years assuming the worst at every turn. Each journey would surely cause her harm. Every experience that meant leaving the house was tempting fate.

When her parents relocated states for her mother's new job and she knew she had to fly for the first time, Rhea had spent many nights awake and fearful imagining just how she would die on that plane. The daydreams weren't necessarily consistent. A shorn-off wing here. An exploded engine there. A deranged pilot flying straight into a mountain. Some nights, a terrorist with a belt full of explosives stood up beside her and screamed that they would all die that day for a varied cause that depended on which extremists the news had reported on that week. There was only one thing she knew for certain. If she got on that plane, she would never get off.

And at twelve years old she had no free will. Ushered forward by her parents with nowhere else to go, she boarded in tears, clutching her favourite teddy although she knew to anyone watching she was too old for such a crutch. More fool them, her brain insistently whispered. If any one of the multiple scenarios that played out in her brain actually happened, the adults who gave her sympathetic but embarrassed glances would wish they had brought their childhood teddies along, too.

Taxiing and take-off had brought her nothing short of abject terror. The sudden crushing whir of the engines. The speed and the unexplained mechanical screams and shrieks within the wings. The sudden slamming of her back into the seat as the aeroplane lifted, up, up, up...surely at any moment they were going to tumble down, down and down. It banked sharply, the land far below filling her window. She had cried out, certain this was the moment they would all perish. But moments later the plane had settled on its path, and she was left with the disapproving and embarrassed shushes from her parents and chuckles from the seasoned flyers around her. A kindly flight attendant had noticed her tears and had crouched down by her seat. The woman had a beaming smile and shiny red lipstick. Rhea had thought of those lips forming the words, "If I don't look worried, there's nothing for you to worry about," for the rest of the journey.

It would be seven more years before she would conceive of flying again, her first experience having traumatised her so deeply. As so often happened in life, she found the old saying, "It's not *what* you know but *who* you know," to change her outlook and the trajectory of her career.

While working at a bar one night, she met Barry Dangerfield, a man whose two names were juxtaposed.

There was nothing sexual about their chat, but Rhea

had been instantly drawn to the kindly older man, whose ice-blue eyes were ringed with deep wrinkles that indicated wisdom rather than substance abuse or a life spent outdoors. Barry's hands were steady and sure, and when he handed over bills or swooped to lift his glass, Rhea marvelled at how strong and capable he seemed. So much so that she asked him what he did.

"I'm a pilot." Barry Dangerfield had plucked his wallet from his hip and flipped it open, showing his private pilot's pass. "I flew commercially for years, but now I've retired I only fly private."

"I'm terrified to fly," Rhea had said, pulling a face.

Looking genuinely baffled, Barry slipped his wallet back in his pants and asked, "Whyever would you be afraid to do something so safe?"

"Hurtling into the air and down again at hundreds of miles an hour doesn't seem so safe to me."

"Safer than working in this bar, mark my words."

As though it was a movie, a fight had erupted behind them. The third that week.

Barry Dangerfield had waited until the fracas was over, then had spent hours talking Rhea through every aspect of flying. He explained how engineering and maintenance evolved to keep its passengers as safe as possible. How training meant that, even if engines blew or holes formed in the cabin, the pilot could usually get you home safe. "Most important of all", he'd said, "the cabin crew will always put you first. And I trusted every member of my crew with every soul on the plane, every damn time."

Something in his words reminded her of that flight attendant with the shiny red lips. That week, much to her surprise, she found herself impulsively booking a flight. A year later, with three more short-haul holidays in the bank, she'd applied to become a flight attendant.

Somewhere over Greenland, dawn brought the sun up from where it had hidden beyond the horizon. For the Vegas to Amsterdam flight, the airline had begun to use automatic filters in the windows. Pull-down blinds were now obsolete, and passengers pushed a button to darken or brighten the glass as they saw fit. Through the blue-tinged filtered window, the rising sun looked purple, a fact that never failed to creep Rhea out a little. She watched the unnatural hue of the orb for a few moments, then shook herself out of her unease and moved to go back to work.

Three quick bursts of light erupted in the cabin.

Somewhere near the back of the plane, Rhea heard screams.

Her training instantly kicked in and she rushed towards the sound of panic.

Anna, another member of the cabin crew, was standing in the aisle, numbly watching a vacant seat. Around the empty chair, passengers were twisted and braced against the seatbacks, hands poised over their seat belts as if ready to unclip them at any moment. *An animal loose on board?* Rhea's mind suggested. *An accident involving bodily fluid that hadn't yet reached her nostrils?*

But neither of those scenarios would cause Anna to freeze in the way she had. Like Rhea, Anna was primed to act. Rhea had seen her colleague in action more than once, dealing competently with a heart attack on board and a moment of extreme turbulence that sent the food cart smashing into a passenger's leg, gouging it open. Anna hadn't faltered, even when the heart attack passenger had slipped away under her clasped palms. Even when the cut-leg passenger had spat at her and threatened to sue.

So, Rhea stared at Anna who gawped at the vacated chair, the seatbelt neatly fastened, and tried to think of any scenario that would have her fellow crew looking so spooked.

"What happened?" she whispered, trained to keep her voice low and measured to avoid alarming the passengers around them.

Anna, apparently forgetting that part of training, raised a trembling finger to the seat and said, "He vanished."

"He *what?*" a woman on the row next to Rhea exclaimed, whipping around to try and see what was going on behind her. Thankfully, most of the other passengers had their earbuds in and were absorbed in movies, shows, and games displayed on the backs of the seats in front of them.

But there were mutterings.

There was growing attention.

Shit.

She grabbed Anna's wrist and tugged her to the galley, dashing the flimsy curtain closed behind them. Standing between the toilet cubicles and the inflatable slide bustle, Rhea dropped Anna's wrist and placed the hand on her upper shoulder. It was a gesture she often used with frantic passengers, doubling as both a comforting measure and a subliminal urge for them to calm down. "Anna. Tell me what happened."

Anna opened her mouth to speak, her eyes still wide with terror. She disappeared.

The second Rhea's fingers lost purchase on her arm and touched her own thumb, her brain replayed the incomprehensible moment when her friend left the space she had been occupying. One moment, Anna was in front of Rhea in the galley. As she peered into her eyes, they were no longer there, and Rhea was left staring at the *Toilet Vacant* sign.

Her heart stepped up to overdrive, making her slightly dizzy. The galley phone rang. She reached out and snatched it up, relishing the feeling of something solid in her palm.

Morgan was working the front of the plane with Ellie. His voice was clipped with irritation, "Rhea, what are you and Anna doing back there? Our trolley's out of Cokes and we need more of the brownies. Ellie said your pax are upset about something and neither of you are there."

"Something's happened," Rhea told him, the wobble in her voice betraying her confusion and fear.

"Which code?" Morgan snapped to business, and Rhea imagined him perusing the plane, on the hunt for threats.

"There isn't a code for this!" Rhea hissed. "People are gone. Anna's gone."

"You aren't making sense. I'm coming down." The phone clicked off, but Rhea kept hold of the handset, unwilling to let it go. The phone was attached to the plane and felt like an anchor keeping her tethered to the craft.

But if the first passenger had vanished the way Anna said they had, not even a seatbelt would have made a difference. The image of the black fabric band and the locked clip lying on the seat darted into Rhea's mind. She staggered a little and tried to convince herself it had been a pocket of turbulence.

The curtain whipped back, and Morgan ducked into the galley, his lip curled in concern and annoyance. His head whipped toward the toilets and, seeing them unoccupied, he asked, "Where the fuck is Anna?"

Behind them came a scream.

Halfway down the plane, the middle row was scattering.

Ellie was hurrying along the aisle, her hands up in a pacifying motion, but the panic of the passengers was escalating.

"She's gone! Linda? *Linda*!" A man screamed at the empty chair beside him. This time, along with the spool of a secured seatbelt, a dropped plastic cup rolled gently on the cushion, spilled wine and half-melted ice cubes scattered across the fabric. The man, middle-aged and comically sunburnt in the shape of the shades he must have worn for his trip to Vegas, stared up at Morgan as though the cabin crew could magically reinstate her.

"We need to tell Captain Waite," Morgan said.

Ellie, a relatively new member of the crew who had only worked short haul before then, was nearest to the cockpit. "I'll go."

Rhea felt a rush of sympathy for the teen. When she had first started, she'd dreaded having to talk to the captain or the co-pilot. It was only when something had gone terribly wrong that she'd sought comfort in the calm and competent voice of the people in the cockpit. Just like Barry Dangerfield, those men and women never rushed. They never panicked. For every situation, they had performed countless simulations and could rely on muscle memory to correct the fault.

However, she doubted any of the pilot's simulations had included vanishing passengers and crew.

Halfway down the aisle, Ellie glanced back, her eyes searching for reassurance. Rhea smiled at Ellie. And the girl was gone.

The cabin erupted in screams of terror.

After seeing a flight attendant vanish, the passengers no longer leapt from their seats. The ones who had jumped from their row after Linda had disappeared hurriedly clambered back into their chairs and cinched their belts so tight Rhea instantly thought of embolism training. A force of habit. *Nobody gives a fuck about embolisms right now*.

Morgan had a strange look on his face. It reminded Rhea of school friends who had discovered the goofiest, silliest magic trick and were waiting for their friend's stunned and impressed reactions. "Is this real?" he said.

Without waiting for Morgan to snap out of it, she took the initiative, striding down the aisle to the cockpit coms. To her right, a man turned his head to look at her with appreciation, then was gone. The seatbelt clanged as it hit the chair, and the passenger who had been seated next to him began to scream, clasping her neck so that her elbows lifted high and stuck up beyond her head in a pose of sheer terror.

Rhea stumbled away from the suddenly empty chair. These people were vanishing instantaneously, with a quiet swiftness of the gentle popping of a detergent liquid bubble. Terror threatened to bring Rhea to her knees but she forced herself to move.

When she reached Dot, she gave her a forced smile. "Everything's okay."

"I heard screaming," the little girl said, her expression requesting no bullshit.

"You did, but you don't have to worry," Rhea reassured her, knowing it was a lie.

Standing up as elegantly as she could, Rhea made her way to the cockpit com.

She depressed the button and requested assistance. Nobody answered.

She waited two minutes, panic growing.

Dot caught her eyes and she remembered her promise: *If the cabin crew aren't worried, you shouldn't be.* Rhea grinned a ridiculous smile that felt somewhat manic.

Still, nobody answered.

Morgan flew to her side, startling her. "Why aren't they answering?"

"I don't know."

He dashed past her to the cockpit door and entered the entrance code.

As Rhea knew, the code didn't automatically grant access. Due to multiple security failings over the years, the pilot and co-pilot had authority over who was given access to the cockpit during flight. The door remained on 'Deny'.

Yet another passenger vanished into oblivion in the

nearest row, leading to the peculiar chinking sound of their neatly buckled belt hitting the unoccupied seat. Rhea avoided Morgan's gaze. Her panic was interrupted by a voice from the cockpit itself.

"Waite disappeared," the voice from co-pilot Sylvain Marin was desolate.

Morgan snatched up the com. "We've entered the code. Let us in."

"Yes, of course. I'm sorry, I just can't understand…"

From the outside, Rhea could hear the co-pilot approach the door. The lock began to move.

Then silence.

"Sylvain? Answer me. Open the door." Morgan's eyes were so wide Rhea could see white all around his green iris. He burst into tears and dropped the com. "They've gone. There's nobody flying the plane."

"Keep your fucking voice down!" Rhea snapped. "We have to stay calm."

"Just how are we supposed to do that, Rhea? We can't get in the fucking cockpit."

"Can you fly a plane?"

"No!"

"Then what difference does it make!"

Her reasoning was the equivalent of a slap to a hysteric. Morgan sagged to the ground, defeated. He peered up at her through his tears. "What are we going to do?"

"Our jobs. We'll just keep the passengers calm until this all blows over."

Morgan's laugh sounded hollow. "Blows over? There is no blowing over in this situation."

Rhea knelt beside him like she would with any

panicked passenger. *Get on their level. Stay calm.* "People have vanished, that's true. But there's nothing to say they won't come back."

Morgan exaggeratedly knocked on the cockpit door. "Oh, Captain, my Captain!"

Snatching his hand, Rhea shushed him, starting to get angry. "Stop that! We don't know what's causing this."

"I do," a small voice came behind them.

Rhea whipped around and found Dot standing at the entrance, her game clutched to her chest. "Go back to your seat and fasten the buckle, sweetie."

"But I know why people are disappearing. I saw them. It's a big silver ship that changes shape. They've been following us since we took off. I thought that they might always be there because nobody else seemed to mind, so I didn't think to worry."

Morgan lunged forward. "You saw *aliens* and you didn't think to worry?"

"Morgan!" Rhea landed a swift kick to his shin, not hard enough to debilitate him but certainly enough to hurt. She ushered Dot back to her seat, a motion that reminded her of when her parents had forced her onto her first plane all those years ago.

One of the scenarios she'd ruminated on back then was something going wrong with the pilots or the controls freezing up. In her terrible daydreams, the plane bounced and shuddered as it hurtled into the mountainside.

Already, the turbulence was increasing as the craft grew closer and closer to the mountains, course unchecked. Rhea only just managed to flip the lock on Dot's belt and tighten it before the plane dipped through a pocket of air, lifting Rhea off the ground for a moment. She gasped, certain she was disappearing, but the kid kept hold of her hand and she soon regained her composure.

Smiling up at her, Rhea froze when Dot pointed to the window.

"They're back again," Dot whispered.

Fear made her muscles resistant to movement. Painfully, Rhea followed the child's gaze and saw a flash of pink light. Dot disappeared, and the Switch console clattered to the floor by Rhea's feet.

"No!"

Crouching, Rhea grabbed at the vacated seat in front of her, the other arm stretching across the aisle in a brace position. The plane jerked and bounced, too near to the mountains.

Three rows up, another passenger vanished into thin air. The woman beside her let out a shrill scream that tore through Rhea's already frayed nerves. She squeezed her fingers into the fabric of the chair. An irrational part of her mind felt that if she hung onto the plane, whatever was taking the passengers and crew wouldn't be able to get enough leverage to take her. But at the same time, a thought just as terrifying, she knew that the craft was heading deeper into the mountain range. And that, unless one or both pilots were returned to the cockpit intact and fully functioning within the next few moments, the plane was going to hit the Watkins Range, and they would all die in any case.

She scrambled into Dot's empty seat, her heel smashing the console screen. Rhea's fingers fumbled, barely managing to open and re-buckle the safety belt. Screams erupted all around her as the passengers suddenly twigged that nobody was steering the ship.

This was the moment all their prayers jumped from wishing that they could stay in their seats, to wanting to take their chances with whatever it was that had stolen their friends away in the blink of an eye.

And then it happened.

The plane tipped onto its side and began to shudder into the slow spiral of stalled engines. Screams and the sudden burst of crumpled metal and exploding fuel tanks flooded Rhea's senses and she clung to her seat. The next moment, her hands grasped nothing.

She was in a dark room. It was so dark, she wondered if this was death. Just a conscious swathe of black for eternity.

But then a red light expanded from the walls around her.

She became aware that she was surrounded, the red blossoming around darkness where bodies stood just feet away from her in a stationary hoop. Smooth, bald heads. Long, gently undulating fingers.

She couldn't move. She was nude, suspended a few feet off the ground by a magnetic pulse.

Through one of the red walls, she caught a glimpse of another room.

More of the stolen passengers were held aloft, unclothed and frozen.

Dot levitated in a hazy glow, her mouth wide open in a terrified cry. When one of the creatures stepped closer to the little girl, Rhea saw its face.

It was worse than anything she'd seen on the X-Files or sci-fi horror movies that portrayed little green men and 'the greys'. It was worse because, instead of shining, baleful black eyes that held little character, their expressions were full of malice. Rhea watched it poke its strange fingers deep into the little girl's mouth, its other hand clasping the back of her neck.

Its arm was forced deep into Dot's throat.

Tears spilled down Rhea's cheeks. She wanted to speak gentle, coaxing rationalities to the girl but was unable to talk, let alone get close enough for her to hear her. She would have said, "It's okay. When people are abducted by aliens they get returned. They always make it back after a while. Back to the place they were taken from..."

The pacifying thought dwindled in Rhea's mind.

The place where they had been taken from no longer existed. The plane had been pulverised against a mountainside.

There was nowhere for the beings to return them *to*.

A hand with fingers the length of pens and the texture of chewed, wet rawhide slapped over her face. The shadowy creature came closer and she saw it in the feint red glow, its eyes showing pure delight in her terror. The long fingers withdrew, and it touched its own face swiping her tears across its thin lips. It smiled a wicked grin.

The room erupted in what she only assumed was a gleeful, rousing, battle cry.

The creatures moved in.

Crashing into the mountain had once been Rhea's deepest, darkest fear. One that had kept her awake at night all those years ago. Now, as the strange-fleshed fingers poked and prodded her naked body, delving into places that she didn't like anyone to see—not for inquiry or to learn about us, as people who believed had speculated for years—but for sheer, masochistic fun, Rhea knew one thing.

She wished she had gone down with the plane.

Through the strange oblong windows, galaxies whizzed by, the stars tinted purple through the glass.

Fallen Eagles and Aces

Time was moving as fast as the horses pulling the convoy of wagons through Devil's Gold Canyon. A hoard of Fallen Eagles flanked the cavalcade on both sides. One moment Langston was reaching out with both hands and preventing Henry Scott from slipping down the side of the wagon's canvas. Less than a second later, Lang was holding the man's severed arms. Blood spurted from the stumps, shorn clean through at the thickest part of Scott's forearms. Langston cringed away from the spurting geysers and dropped the limbs. One of them tumbled and bounced away over the canopy, leaving a streak of red against the canvas. The other arm remained stuck flat against Lang's trigger hand. He glanced down at it in confusion and found that the fat old man's fingers had slid under his knife holster, the tycoon's ostentatious rings snagged against the leather and leaving them palm-to-palm, his sheared wrist completely covering Langston's hand and stopping him from going for his gun.

The Fallen Eagle that had disarmed Scott began to clamber up the front of the canvas, its claws tearing into the thick material. Inside the carriage, Lady Scott let out a horrified squeal. Lang's Whitworth rifle, stowed at his thigh, was within what should have been easy grasp. He tried to shake the disembodied arm from his own, but every time he shook his hand the ring twisted deeper into the leather strap that held his Green River knife, the weapon's hilt trapping the rapidly blueing flesh of the dead man's digits between leather and gold.

The monster snorted, its head rising over the domed white of the sand-speckled tarp. Langston let out a yell and stumbled back, his backside bouncing against the curved fabric. He was almost propelled down to the ground and under the wheels of the cart, but he scrabbled against the canvas with his one free hand, the other uselessly pawing with the dead man's stump and smearing dark gobbets of already congealing blood on the wagon's roof. The Fallen Eagle's clawed hand struck out and tore into the cart, puncturing the tight canopy between Lang's shins. The monster raised itself up, and fear shrank Lang's bowels. Fallen Eagles looked like a dog and lizard crossed rather than bird, and the 'eagle' moniker had been given to them because of the gold flecks that peppered their flesh. They were the reason why men paid mercenaries like Langston and his gang a fortune to escort them to the creek in Devil's Gold Canyon, where the panning was the key to riches beyond anyone's wildest fancy. An Eagle was slang for a ten-dollar gold coin, and each of the monsters could have paid out enough to keep a man in finery for life. That was the thing that always baffled Langston; the damned fools who dared even attempt to pan in the creek were already wealthy as any man could dream. Otherwise, they wouldn't be able to pay for people like Lang and his crew to protect them while they attempted the trip through Fallen Eagle territory. Along with the shimmers of finest gold, the creatures' skin was the deep dark grey of a sky falling into an early winter's night. The flesh ruched up where their four lizard-like limbs met body, shoulders and hips in line with the peak of their lithe backs. An Eagle's spine tapered out into a thin tail that was as long as its body. Golden claws tipped four long fingers on each paw. Their faces were snouted and sleek, black eyes positioned high and central above a mouth that split into grotesque rows of small, razor teeth that looked like a few dozen knife tips clipped and lodged higgledy-piggledy in the creatures' grey and gold gums.

Now, the monster opened wide, showing torn shirt and lingering strips of flesh left by the fat tycoon's arms.

Clinging onto the wagon's canopy so he wasn't bucked free, Langston couldn't get to his gun—his efforts were thwarted by the limb that was outstaying its welcome. He could do nothing but fight with what he had to hand. And all he had to hand was the severed stump of Scott's arm that was stuck fast to his own. Langston let fly, screaming and swinging. The flesh of the open wound struck the Fallen Eagle against the side of what might be its cheek – the slender space between its eye and the height of its inner jaw that was always the best spot for a bullet or a knife. It flinched, then opened its mouth and let out a piercing screech. Lang stared down its throat, at the bands of grey flesh lined with serrated points, the sparkling gold that shimmered over its forked tongue.

Lang gave one last feeble attempt at attack, willing the dead fingers to disengage from the knife strap as he whacked Scott's stump against the Eagle's head. His only other option was to let go of the canopy with his other hand and reach for his pistol, or the Green River knife that Scott's severed hand was helpfully pointing to, the blade in its usual position strapped against the length of Lang's forearm. But that would mean sliding closer to the creature without any purchase or knowledge of which way his body would start falling, or—perhaps worse—send him tumbling straight off the side under the convoy's hooves with only one free hand to try and stop his descent.

The Fallen Eagle reared up, neck elongating as it stretched over him. The mouth widened, its jaws unhinging as it sized him up. Lang stared up at the hypnotic gold and black within the depths of its throat, then fell backwards against the tarp as a deep red hole exploded in the centre of its jaw.

Tabitha leapt from the canopy of the wagon beside his, her heavy landing almost dislodging his fingers from the tarp. She scrambled to her feet, her movements jostling the fabric so Lang had to brace with his legs and pray he wasn't flung from the convoy like a flicked gnat. She fired again, the booming barrel of her sawed-off Winchester causing the frenzied horses below to run even faster. The monster, its head nothing but a black pulp, slid away and was trampled under wheels and hooves. Gold speckles glittered in the dark blood that trickled down the dusty canvas.

Tabitha glared down at Langston, the look on her face

somewhere halfway between puzzled and disgusted. "Just what in the hell are you doing?"

He sat, sweat sluicing down his back, and blinked up at her. He lifted his arm to show her his predicament, only the damn dead man's hand suddenly decided to relinquish its grip on the strap and the stump tumbled away over the side of the canvas top before she could see it.

"You know you've got a rifle, right?" Tabitha sneered, and Lang had no time to explain or to thank her for saving his hide before she'd taken a flying leap and jumped onto the roof of the carriage to the left, shooting at a Fallen Eagle that was flanking them after cutting through the mountain range. They were getting sneakier.

Langston finally tugged his Whitworth from its strap, the cool weight a familiar and welcome sensation against his numbed fingers. The additional girth of Scott's digits pushing into the leather band of his knife holster had squeezed his wrist until his fingers were almost as blue as Scott's own would be in no time at all, but when he tested his trigger finger it answered the call.

He turned to survey his crew and saw Harlan was struggling to keep the last of the wagons secure, three of the monsters fast advancing on the slowing horses. The young man was leaning over the side of the wagon top, his mop of dark hair plastered across his eyes as he fired a few rounds, striking the sand at the feet of the nearest Eagle.

Langston levelled his weapon and shot through the creature's forehead. Harlan's next bullet took out another. The boy scrambled to reload. A creature clambered onto the roof beside him, and Harlan quickly stuck the empty gun in his pants and whipped out his blade. When the monster leapt to pin him, Harlan jabbed upwards, driving the knife into its guts. He kicked, sending the body back over the edge of the wagon.

Resighting his Whitworth, Lang took a pot shot at the last of the creatures that was advancing through the sand. The Fallen Eagle tumbled away, its tail lashing up clouds of dust as it spun. It wasn't dead. Lang knew he'd only punctured its shoulder. But he tracked it with the barrel of the rifle until the convoy was beyond the danger zone where the Fallen Eagles regularly seemed to swarm from nowhere. As the wagons trundled away toward the creek the creature licked its wound with its forked tongue. It watched them leave, sculking like a scolded dog. Langston had a creeping feeling he'd see it again.

Throckmorton let out a whoop and pumped a thick, freckled fist into the air, then slid down the tarp and snatched up the reins of the horses that were leading the convoy. Sweat streaked white on their flanks, and their eyes were wide and white-edged with terror. Froth bubbled around their bits. Throck gave the reins a yank and after a few hundred yards the procession stumbled to a halt.

Lady Scott stepped out of the lead wagon and snapped her head up to find Langston, who was sitting astride the canopy with his rifle held across the width of his body. Now that he was free to hold it, he didn't feel much like letting go. The woman shielded her eyes from the sun and glowered up at him, "Mr Langston, you failed your mission."

Lang sniffed and stared down at the new widow, who was handling her updated marital status better than most he'd seen. "How you figure?"

"Your task was to bring us to the creek safe and sound. My husband is no longer with us. Therefore, you have failed."

"Now then, Mrs Scott. I clearly instructed your husband to stay inside the wagon with you. If he'd done as he was told you'd all be sittin' pretty right here. That ain't any doing of mine."

Lady Scott's chin trembled for a fraction of a second, but the old dame found her grit and firmed her jaw. "Henry Scott was a proud man, Mr Langston. He would never sit by and let another man fall without making an attempt to save him."

Langston opened his mouth to explain how her dumb husband had almost been the cause of his demise—him and his infernal stumped arm—but Tabitha hopped down off the roof of the cart she was astride and slipped her Arkansas Toothpick against the woman's throat before he could answer.

Lady Scott swallowed, her throat working against the blade, and lifted her slender fingers up to rest splayed but still on her collarbone in composed defeat.

Tabitha spoke low and steady close to the old girl's ear, and before Lang could work out what the end game might be, Lady Scott was nodding, the knife was lowered, and the woman reached into the cart and tugged out a sack of cash.

Langston pushed off the wagon and stumbled in the rocks, but caught the sack when Tabitha flung it to him.

The dame looked to Lang, haughty but appeased. "And where do we camp?"

"Around the bend, follow the river. Remember all of you, the creek is no more safe than the plain we just rode through durin' the hours of dusk and dawn, so no panning for gold until tomorrow. We'll watch over the creek and keep you as safe as possible 'til then. And right now, I can escort you to the camp, Ma'am."

"I no longer have any need of your services" Scott bit back. She reached into the cart and hauled out a roll of her belongings, struggling to tug it over her shoulders. She set off trudging toward the panning creek, the other members of her party following solemnly behind.

"Wait-" Langston opened the sack and pulled out a handful of bills. He held them out to her and lowered his chin. "Since I didn't get you all over safe."

That steely old woman, she stared him right in the eye and slapped the money out of his hand like he was a kid with a pocketful of worms. She spun on her heel and kept on walking.

Throckmorton let out a hoot of laughter. "Another satisfied customer."

Lang reached down into the dust and picked up the bills before they blew away on the evening breeze that was working its way through the canyon. His arm felt crusty where the gore of the old timer's wrist had squirted onto his flesh and dried quick in the sun. When he patted off the bills and put them back in the sack, flakes of copper tumbled down to earth along with the scattering dust of the sands.

Harlan wandered toward them from the back of the convoy, looking a little dishevelled after the taxing run.

He went over to Throckmorton and gestured to his shoulder. "Did it get me?"

Face falling in concern, Throckmorton's huge hands tugged Harlan's shirt to the side and started to inspect the skin of the younger man's chest. "There's a scratch."

"A scratch or a bite?" Tabitha enquired; thumb primed to arch back the lever on her sidearm.

"I think it's just a scratch. Its nail caught me when I cut its belly," Harlan told her, the panic in his large dark eyes betraying the calm of his voice.

Throckmorton smoothed the skin with his palm, tenderly, instinctively moving his body to protect Harlan. It didn't take much – Throck was a ginger bear of a man, while Harlan's lithe frame could fit behind him three times over. "He's fine. It's a scratch and barely even that."

Tabitha's fingers flexed, but she moved them away from the gun and instead hooked her thumb into her belt loop. "Lucky for you."

"For all of us," Throck said, forcefully. Behind him, Harlan leaned forward and nuzzled his forehead into the ranger's back.

Langston scanned his crew—God dammit, there weren't many of them now—and regarded how beat up they all looked. The day wasn't over yet. They weren't just hired to transport wealthy gold-hunters through the monster-infested canyon and into the creek. It was also their job to watch the creek itself, to monitor the panners sifting there and make sure they weren't jumped as they hunted for the precious gold that came straight from the bodies of the creatures that were set on killing them. It was some strange poetry, this existence at

Devil's Gold Canyon, and the odd humour of it wasn't lost on Langston. He just took each day, each challenge, as it came. Tried to make sure as many of his crew came out of the day as unscathed as he could. "Tabi, you n' me are on first watch tonight."

Tabitha nodded. Although she looked a little tired, she accepted the direction without question or qualm. She was his finest soldier and had been with him since day one. Throckmorton grinned at Harlan, who looked about ready to collapse with relief at getting a break. The kid was a great knifeman, but as the newest member of the team he didn't have as much experience or stamina as the others.

"Let's head up to camp." Langston said.

They trudged toward the trail that led to their usual campsite, a bluff that gave them the best aerial view of the creek bed. Although the panners knew not to come to the creek at night, sometimes greed got the better of them. The idea of getting the hop on the other people in the convoy and finding the best of the gold somehow lured the foolhardy out during prime Eagle hunting hours. Lang loved the idea of finding gold as much as any man. But weighed up against the thought of being chomped to death by a Fallen Eagle, it was no contest. And death wasn't the worst of it, he knew all too well. If an Eagle managed a bite that didn't kill a man right away, they'd wish for a bullet all too soon. He shuddered at the thought and tried to push it from his mind.

There was a sudden scurrying through the brambles to the side of the pathway, and all four members of Lang's crew whipped towards it, pistols raised.

An old man in filthy-looking long-johns staggered out onto the dusty track and beamed a gap-toothed grin. "The King himself!" he declared, looking Lang up and down. "Or, should that be, the defeater of the Golden King?"

Tabitha let out a breathy cuss and holstered her weapon. "You again."

The old timer gave a brief bow and hopped from foot to foot. "You'll be savin' the country soon, mark my words."

Throckmorton yawned loudly, keeping his shotgun pointed at the old man. "Can I just shoot him so we can be done with this?"

Lang laughed but shook his head. The old man had been making a regular appearance at camp, babbling about the end of the world, and singing *The Unfortunate Rake*. He seemed harmless enough, though. Lang didn't mind humouring him. "Can I help you?"

"You'll help us all! The monsters are in the *rock itself.* Right over there!" The vagrant turned and pointed with a dirt-covered, gnarled finger. He was gesturing to a wall of the canyon on the far side of the creek. "You can walk straight through when the doorway opens."

"Sure, you can," Tabitha rolled her eyes. "That'll save us some time next time we have to ramble back to the township."

Harlan laughed, leaning sleepily against Throck's side.

The crew were too tired for this, Lang knew. As much as he kind of enjoyed the old man's rantings, he figured he'd better move him out the way before patience wore out and he took a bullet. "Well, if I can't be helpin' you, we're just gonna move on by. Alright?"

The man stepped aside, but as Lang made to move past him, he snatched out and grabbed at Lang's chest.

Instinctively, he clasped the old man's wrist, ready to hurl him into the bracken if he had to. But the crazy old varmint had taken a liking to Lang's necklace, clasping the piece of obsidian stone that hung there.

"A gift!" the old man stared, wide eyed. He released the necklace and nodded his head. "Find the Golden King, before the swarm takes over. The gift will save the whole dang country!"

Tabitha eyed Lang as the old timer let out a whoop and dashed away back into the bracken, the strains of him singing "*There goes an unfortunate lad to his hooooome....*" fading into the distance. "You alright?"

Although the question seemed ironic, Lang guessed he must have looked a little rattled. He touched the necklace, making sure the crazy old loon hadn't snatched away with it, and nodded. Old timer was crazy enough to dig for water in an outhouse, but the thing was, the necklace *was* a gift. From a tribe leader Lang had helped out years before. He ran his thumb along the dull edge of the mock blade and let out an exasperated sigh. "Ready to save the whole dang country, fellas?"

"Ugh, I'm ready to sleep for a thousand years. How about that instead?" Harlan answered, practically leaping the last few yards to where their campfire and bedrolls were waiting for them.

"Bet you're glad we're on watch, huh?" Lang pointed out, and Throck slapped him on the shoulder gratefully as he followed behind Harlan, the older man as eager to reach their shared bedroll as the younger.

Lang let Tabi move on before him, and he glanced back to see if the crazy vagrant was still lurking. But they were alone. He let go of the necklace and headed up to the bluff.

Throckmorton threw himself down next to Harlan and yawned, stroking a hand over his thick red moustache. "I'm beat."

Harlan turned onto his side to face him and slung an arm over his partner's middle. "I'm takin' the hint, I guess. Straight to sleep, huh?"

Throck beamed and tilted his head, kissing Harlan on the temple. He settled back down and was snoring in moments.

Langston sat at the cliff's edge, his attention alternating between the creek below and Tabitha. She sat a couple of metres off to his right, propped against a rock with her arm hanging crooked over her raised knee, her pistol trailing from her pointer finger. She glanced over her shoulder at the two men cuddled up together by the campfire and smiled when the steady grating of Throckmorton's snores rose over the sound of the crackling fire.

"I guess Harlan's shit outta luck tonight," she muttered, tossing her head toward the sleeping pair.

"Sure looks that way. Saves us an earful of things we don't rightly need to hear, though."

Tabitha chuckled. "You got that right."

Langston stared across at the woman, watched as she angled her throat up and breathed in the scent of the evening. The setting sun cast a peachy glow across her neck and made her dark hair seem auburn. Langston swallowed and scooched a little closer to her. "It's kinda nice though, ain't it. Them two being together I mean."

A small hum of agreement came from Tabitha's glowing throat.

"I mean, it gets pretty lonesome on these missions. Any day now, those monsters could get the better of us. Makes a man think."

"Makes a man think he should fight with a gun instead of another man's arm?" Tabitha darted an eyebrow and cut her gaze toward him.

Langston felt a blush heat his cheeks and gave a breathy laugh. "Just, it makes a man think he might not want to die out here alone. Don't you ever feel that way?"

Tabitha leaned forward and scraped at a dried clod of dirt on the heel of her boot with her knife. "I like being on my own. I know what I'm doing this for. How I wanna live my life. There's no distractions when it's just me. Makes me a better fighter."

Edging a little closer, Langston watched her dislodge the dirt and holster her weapon back at her hip. He licked his lips, willing her to look up at him. She kept her eyes fixed on the creek below. The water reflected the pinked sky, making it look like a thin ribbon of the sky itself had fluttered down to earth. A discarded pan lay tilted on the silty bank, a pinprick of reflected sun blazing like a lone diamond. "But don't you ever get that feeling toward another? Like Throck and Harlan over there? I mean, we knew from the day Harlan joined us that Throck had eyes for nobody else. You don't ever feel that way?"

Finally, she regarded him, her face casting shadows over itself now it was turned from the sun. "I ain't never felt that way, Lang. Not about a man. Not about a woman.

I guess I'm just wired a little different than most folks, that's all."

Langston's jaw fell, and he closed his mouth in a hurry to try and disguise his shock and disappointment. "You never felt like you wanted to be close to nobody?"

She shook her head, amusement in her eyes. "Never have, never will. But I'm kind of glad in a way. It's just me, myself, and I. I think I'm doin' a pretty good job of it."

"That you are." Langston shook his head and blew air through pursed lips. He didn't know what to say. He had always had urges toward females throughout his life, from early in his childhood until now, where he spent his night imagining laying on his bedroll with Tabitha in his arms. It had never even occurred to him that some people just didn't feel that way for anyone, and never would. He realised Tabitha was watching him hard, scrutinising his expression. He forced a huge smile, "Well, that's just...aces."

"Aces?"

She was humouring him, goading him to say something offensive, but he wouldn't bite. His pride was hurt, but he knew there was no point in pursuing the matter with her. He scooted back to the left, making a show of trying to get a better view of the creek below. "Sure. Hell, you know exactly who you are and what you want and nobody's going to come in and confuse that. Ain't that a less complicated life than most."

Her eyes widened in surprise at his casual acceptance. She opened her mouth to answer him, when a piercing scream echoed up through the canyon.

"What the hell was that?" Lang jumped to his feet, on

high alert.

Behind them, Throckmorton snorted and sat up. He smoothed a hand over Harlan's hair, gently waking him. "Something's afoot," he grunted, slapping his own cheeks and reaching for his shotgun.

Tabitha crawled forward, peering over the edge. "I don't see anything."

Lang scanned the ground below. Now that the sun had fallen even lower, the creek had lost its pinkish tone. It looked dull and murky green. He scanned the shale and froze, his hairs standing up. "The pan's gone."

"Huh?"

"There was a pan layin' down there on the creek side. It's gone." It could only mean that a person had been down there. Outside of curfew. Luring the creatures from the canyon.

"Shit." Tabitha jumped to a standing position and yanked her gun from the holster, checking the magazine. She strode past the campsite, heading for the trail down to the water. "Come on, waddies!" she called over her shoulder.

Bleary eyed, Harlan shrugged on his jacket and let Throck haul him to his feet.

Throckmorton cocked his gun and grinned at Langston. "You heard the lady, come on, waddy!"

"She was talking to you..." Langston gritted out, but Throck had already set off in a trot, excited for battle.

Lang took one last look down at the creek, scanning for Eagles but seeing none. Pensive, he began to follow, but noticed that Harlan was hesitating. The boy's face looked ashen. "You comin'?"

"Of course, I'm coming," Harlan frowned. He lifted

his handgun to load it and fumbled with the magazine, spilling bullets across his bedroll. Cussing, he scrambled to collect them with trembling fingers.

Impatient, Lang strode over and snatched the gun from him, plucking the bullets from his palm and filling the magazine. "There. What the hell's wrong with you?"

"Bad dream, I guess," Harlan swallowed.

Another scream rang out through the canyon. While the first scream had sounded human, this one did not.

"Well, you woke up in a nightmare, kid. Let's go down there and see what's what." Langston broke into a run, eager to join Tabi and Throck at the bank of the creek. He slid down the pathway, rolling the sleeve of his duster up so he had sight of the knife strapped to his wrist. He clutched his Whitworth, the long slender barrel braced over his forearm as he picked his way down the path, and the comforting weight of his LeMat bounced against his thigh. But, like Harlan, he was a knifeman deep down. His Green River had saved his hide with seconds to spare on more occasions than he'd have liked to admit.

When he made it down to the clearing, Throck was already splashing through the creek, kicking up silt and gold with his huge boots. A Fallen Eagle was poised to strike, its tongue darting out of the side of its lipless mouth. Throck lifted his shotgun and blasted the top of its head off.

One of the members of the Scott convoy was cowering in the bracken at the bottom of the path. He looked up at Lang and pointed with a trembling hand. "He...he got bit."

Lang followed the finger and saw the sifting pan that he'd spotted from the bluff, dropped in the silt of the embankment. Tatters of torn shirt draped over the top of it, and spots of deep red blood that gave way to thick, tar-like black streaked along the embankment. Footprints faded into drag marks that worked their way around a boulder. A Fallen Eagle blundered from around the rock face, its claws stomping through the footsteps that had been left in the silt. This one was ungainly, its movements irregular, and Lang knew it was the prospector who'd just been attacked. One bite from a Fallen Eagle, you'd better wish you died quick. If not, this was your fate. A bullet from Lang's Whitworth ended the man's suffering.

Tabi gave a shout, a warning to Throckmorton. The burly man whipped round and pulled the trigger as an Eagle appeared out of nowhere, practically leaping right on top of him.

"What in the-"

"It came out of the rock!" Tabi gasped, incredulous. She gawped as another creature materialised, first its snout, then its shoulders pulled through the undulating mountainside.

Throck strode up to it and smashed the barrel of his heavy shotgun down into the soft space under its eye. Its skull caved in, and chucks of black flesh spattered his arm. He lifted the gun again and pummelled down for good measure, then spat on the carcass at his feet.

Distracted by his crew members' shouts about the rock, Lang didn't realise that the young prospector who'd been crouched at the foot of the path had been covering a bite of his own.

"Watch out!" Harlan warned, pushing Lang to the side as the newly-born Fallen Eagle sprang from the bracken. Blades in his hands, Harlan struck out with a roundhouse kick, knocking the monster to the ground.

"Thanks!" Lang rushed to the side to take care of another of the creatures that appeared as if from nowhere. This time, he whipped his Green River from his wrist holster, tossing it so it whipped handle over blade and stuck fast in the creature's ear.

Lang strode up to the dying creature and reached down, twisting the knife as he tugged it from the skull. He wiped gold-speckled black goo on his pants with satisfaction. Looking back at Harlan, Lang frowned. The boy was still in a tussle with the freshly created Fallen Eagle. One of his blades had been lost in the scuffle, and the other arm and knife was wedged underneath him as the creature forced its weight onto Harlan's chest.

Harlan let out a cry as the monster's jaws bit deep into his shoulder.

Throck yelled his name and scrambled over the rocks of the creek, splashing water as he lifted his shotgun and advanced on the creature that was mauling his lover.

Tabitha spun and trailed her gun on the scene, but Throckmorton stepped in front of her sights. His shotgun let out a blast that sent the monster spinning to the side, its razor teeth snatched from Harlan's flesh and sending spatters of blood up into the air in a mini geyser.

Harlan clutched the wound and looked up at Throckmorton, his mouth wide, eyes rounding in terror. "No...no, I don't wanna be like that," he groaned, lowering his hand from the gash to brace himself on the ground. As soon as the pressure left the wound, the torn flesh parted to show a thick wash of black that glittered, even in the dying light of the sunset. Harlan crouched on trembling legs and stared at the injury, dumbstruck.

Throckmorton had stopped a few feet away from him, a puzzled look on his face. For once, the gruff ranger had nothing to say. His eyes scanned over his lover, a slight smile twitching the corner of his mouth. It was as though his brain were trying to make sense of what had happened and was protecting him from the truth by convincing him it was all a big joke.

Harlan met Throck's eyes, and the blood drained from his face. He hunched as if he'd just taken a punch to the gut, then started tearing at his shirt, gasping for air. He pulled apart the material, buttons scattering into the shale of the creek. His chest looked creamy and toned, and for a second they all stared, waiting. But then something under his skin began to undulate, to the left of his right nipple. Another pulsing mass rushed from the wound at his shoulder, striking sideways as if it were making a beeline for his heart. Harlan let out a scream of pain through gritted teeth.

"Oh, darlin'" Throckmorton gasped, dropping his gun and striding forward with open arms.

"Don't touch him!" Tabitha barked, stepping between them.

Throck gawped at her, his face contorting from despair to fury. "I have to go to him!"

"He'll kill you in a few moments, sure as look at you."

"Tabi!" The stricken boy wailed behind her, distraught.

She moved so she was sideways between the two men, gun held at her thigh, ready to use it on either of them should they come at her. "I'm sorry, kid, but we know the score. We all saw it happen with the prospectors just now, just as we've seen it a hundred times. That gold is in your blood. It's turning you. Ain't nothing we can do."

"She's right!" Langston called. He was a few metres away, scrabbling to reload his rifle, on high alert for any more beasts. Especially since his entire team was either distracted or dying. *Shit. He'd lost another one.*

Harlan sobbed, hunched over and clawing at his torso as his blood thickened with the gold flecks. The tears that ran down his cheeks left trails of gleaming yellow. He let out an agonised squeal and reached out a hand to grab Tabitha's arm.

She moved swiftly, twisting out of his range and lifting her pistol in line with his head.

"No!" Throck yelled, his booming voice filling the canyon with its echo.

Tabi frowned, hesitating, her finger twitching over the trigger.

Harlan looked down at his body. The skin was tearing in places, trickles of black blood glistening as they rolled down his skin. It was a pitiful sight. The whites of his eyes were darkening, grey orbs with crusted gold that stuck to his lashes. He looked up at Throck, helpless. "She's right," he whispered, his throat scratchy. He gave a hacking cough and spat blood and glitter onto the ground at his feet. "I don't wanna be one of them."

Throck stared at him. "I don't wanna lose you."

"It *hurts*, Throck," Harlan gasped, a fresh slew of ever-thickening tears pulsing down his cheeks. A cut opened up on his jawbone, showing a sliver of white between the darkness that was fast replacing his blood and the shimmering gold specks pulsing agonisingly through his veins.

Langston gave a final check that there were no more Eagles advancing and felt satisfied the coast was clear. He holstered his rifle and stepped toward his crew. Seeing him approach, Harlan tried to toss his knife to the leader, hoping that he would take on the task of ending his suffering with his own weapon. But the kid's hands were as weak as a kitten with a broken leg, and his trusty knife slipped straight through his fingers and landed in the blood-spattered ground at his feet.

In a gesture of sympathy, Lang put a hand gently on Throckmorton's shoulder. The large man seemed to fold inward at the touch, his broad shoulders rounding, his arms reaching toward the ground.

Harlan shuddered, his lips baring around blackening gums. Dark blood painted his teeth. He looked to Tabi. "Please. Do it."

Tabitha nodded, raising the gun to aim at his temple.

The shotgun blast took them all by surprise.

Throckmorton's rounds hit Harlan square in the chest. Harlan didn't fall back with a hole in his front, the way a normal man would who'd been shot with a Coach shotgun. Instead, the boy who was more than half beast at that point exploded into gold dust. Dark spatters of thick blood and tatters of his ruined clothes fell to the bank edge. Following the trail of the smoke from Throck's gunshot, a burst of gold speckles moved with the breeze and drifted over the creek.

Langston watched the spectacle, moved to awe despite the circumstance. The gold flakes swarmed like a flock of fall birds then scattered, sinking beneath the babbling waters. Days—hell, perhaps even years from now—the miners would be shaking what was left of Harlan through their pans, delighting at the haul of gold amongst the silt.

Throckmorton covered his face with his hands and sobbed, his huge back jumping.

Tabi buckled her weapon and bowed her head. "I sure am sorry, Throck. He was a good 'un, and he was yours."

Lang strode to the kid's dropped knife and picked it up in his handkerchief, wiping slicks of blood—black, red, and gold—from the hilt. When it was clean, he slid the knife into his boot and dropped the gore-soaked material. He gave Tabi a half-smile as she came to him, moved by her kind words to the big man.

The woman's expression changed as she walked, shifting from sympathy to business. She inclined her head toward the rock face where the monsters had lumbered through the wall. "I never thought that crazy old loon was tellin' the truth about that mountain, but you saw it yourself, right?"

Nodding, Langston followed her gaze. The rock looked almost normal, but if you squinted real hard, a strange glow pulsed around the area where the Fallen Eagles had emerged. "Makes you almost wonder if he's right about the other things, too."

"You read my mind," Tabi's eyes grew sharp, and they both started to walk toward the mountain.

They came to a halt a couple of feet in front of it, tentative. From what they'd seen, and what the old timer had told them, any number of Eagles was waiting to pounce from within the rock face. Somehow. It was crazy, Lang knew that. But he had seen them emerge as if the wall wasn't even there.

Impulsively, he struck out an arm, half-hoping his fingers would clash against solid rock. Instead, the back of his hand vanished, blurring into the reddish boulders.

"What the hell..." Lang stared in dumb fascination at the undulating rock and snatched his hand back from the swirling mass. He gasped and brought his palm up to his eyes, panicked, but his fingers were intact.

"What did it feel like?" Tabitha asked, frowning and inspecting the hand.

"It just felt like nothing. Kind of cold, but like an open space or somethin'."

"The old man said we gotta go in the canyon to defeat 'em once and for all, didn't he?"

Lang paused for a moment, staring blankly at the strange swirling rockface. Tabitha kept her gun trailed on the shimmering rocks, knowing full well that there wasn't just the question of them going inside. At any moment, ten of those creatures could come pouring out of there. She glanced back at Throck, who was still squatting with his huge hands covering his face, the fingers clawed into his hair so tight the skin had turned white.

Finally, Lang heaved a deep sigh and nodded to himself. He drew his gun in one hand and plucked the knife from his wrist holster into the other. "If the old man's right, it's worth a try. Right?"

Tabitha met his eyes and pulled a face. "You're trusting that crazy old bastard?"

"If what he said's true there's soon going to be enough of those creatures to take over the whole of America if we don't do something about it."

"You hired me to protect rich folks fixin' to get richer. Didn't say nothin' about savin' the whole damn country." Tabi flicked her eyes to meet Lang's, a wry smile on her lips.

"Well, how's about startin' with savin' our own hides. Because that's what this kettle of snakes boils right down to. I figure, anyway."

Tabi's chin wrinkled as she weighed up their options. She peered back at the creek, and Langston could tell she was contemplating how Harlan must have felt in his final moments. There was no way they could stand by and watch that unleashed on the world. On their families back in the townships.

Tabitha turned back to the rock and gave a decisive nod. "You got matches? I'm guessin' there's a chance it's awful dark in there."

Lang patted his pocket, the match box a comforting edge against his palm. "Sure do. A candle, too. You with me?"

"O' course I am, boss."

"Well, that's just aces," he grinned.

She snorted, her face crumpling into short-lived laughter.

Lang looked to Throckmorton, but Tabitha shook her head. The man was broken, and she knew that having him in the team would make their progress unpredictable at best. Lang took a deep breath and stepped toward the swirling mass of the rockface. Steeling himself, he leaped forward.

Tabitha watched the rock swallow Lang whole, the fluid surface creeping over his back until he was completely consumed by it. One moment Lang had been standing in front of her. Now, he was inside the mountain. She was momentarily stupefied, a visceral reaction of seeing a man defy the natural law of things right in front of her.

Now it was her turn. She reached down and clutched a fistful of dusty earth, letting it trickle through her fingers, grounding her. Ready, she checked her gun and advanced on the strange entranceway.

A hand grabbed her shoulder and gave her a sharp tug.

Throck stared wildly at her, his eyes bloodshot, his hair sticking up in mad tufts. He looked like a man suddenly possessed by a demon. "We're gonna destroy those bastards?"

"We are. Me and Lang. You stay right here an' guard the entrance."

"No way, Tabi! They killed Harlan." A fresh tear sneaked from his eye as he said the words, and for a moment his expression changed from insane rage to disbelief. Within the blink of an eye, the crazy was back. He held his shotgun high. "I'm gonna get every last one of those motherfuckers."

Pushing past her with a shoulder-barge, Throckmorton stepped into the undulating doorway. Halfway through, he stopped. He shuddered.

Tabitha watched as the rock began to harden, firm crags creeping toward the man who was situated half in and half out of the entranceway. His arms snapped tight to his sides as the stone encased him, his feet dragging rivets of earth as the closing canyon pushed his legs to snap together in the middle. The shimmering, glistening strangeness that signalled the mountain's unearthly doorway disappeared. Throckmorton's body shuddered violently once more, then stilled.

Hanging from the rockface, the back of Throck's long leather coat was suspended. Tabi lifted a trembling finger and pushed at it. Inside, a firm but yielding shank of muscular flesh pushed back at her fingertip. The doorway had closed. And it had encased Throck inside it, squashing him flat in the centre.

She staggered backwards, thoughts racing. Did that mean Lang was also squished flat deeper inside the rocks? If she had stepped forward instead of Throck, would *she* have faced the same fate?

She felt a breeze curl over her cheek and tilted her head toward the night sky, suddenly grateful to be alive and outside. She breathed in the dusty scent of the cool night air and listened to the sound of the gold-laced creek babbling over the rocks.

"I done told you!" Came an eager voice right behind her.

She whipped around and found the crazy old man in the stained long johns bouncing up and down on his heels, eagerly.

"He's done it now! Young Langston. What a hero! Gone and saved the whole stinkin' country."

"Alright, old timer," Tabi shook her head, holstering her gun and preparing to move on. She was done with this canyon. Done with gold. Done with monsters. Might take a move out West, she thought to herself. Take on some private bodyguard work.

"Hey there!" The man yelled after her.

She turned, humouring him.

The old loon was smiling, his eyes suddenly as wide and appealing as a foal's. He clasped his hands at his chest, imploring. Something about him looked awfully familiar to her, past the deep lined crags of his skin and shaggy white hair. His beam showed craters where most of his teeth used to be. "Whatever you're headin' off to do, I guess it's just aces."

Aces? Tabitha stared hard. The man in front of her must have been at least 80 years old. But still, there was familiarity in his stature, his lanky limbs sprouting from a long, lean body. The glint in his grey eyes. "Langston?"

The man hopped from foot to foot and let out a whoop, then turned on his heel and dashed away into the bracken, his arms flailing wildly. "He done it! Man's a dang hero!" he yelled as he vanished around the side of the mountain, breaking into song.

Langston crept through the dark tunnel of the cavern, feeling his way along the sides. The blackness around him enhanced his sense of smell and touch. The rocks felt rough as dried snake hide other than the smooth flecks of gold that peppered the surface every now and then. The air smelled of dusty nights and unaired barns that had been locked up for years. There was something else, too. A slight odour of decay, as if the barn had been shut up with a forgotten horse or two inside and all that was left was a pile of bones and some air-dried flesh.

He patted his fingers over the matches in his pocket, the small rectangle a comfort. There must be at least fifty matches in there, he recalled. But he'd save them until he needed them. Lord knew how long he was going to be stuck in the canyon.

He froze at the sound of movement up ahead.

The slithering swish of a Fallen Eagle's tail. It was up ahead of him in the narrow passageway, he guessed around twenty feet or so. He couldn't see in the dark, but he wouldn't put a bet against the creature being able to see him. He put a hand to his wrist holster and slipped out his Green River knife.

He held his breath.

There was a snarl in the darkness. Langston felt rammed in on either side, the walls of the cavern that before had brushed lightly against his upper arms as he strode through it now feeling as though they'd narrowed, clasping him tight in their grasp. He was imagining it, but now that he was heading straight toward an Eagle with barely any room to turn against the rocks, he might as well have been shut inside a two-foot-wide bull stall. He forced his hand to stay steady, holding the knife out in front of his heart. He didn't move a muscle, hoping that the creature would make plenty of noise as it descended on him.

He got his wish.

The Fallen Eagle let out a screech that echoed down the corridor and sent Langston's bowels raw, a shudder pulsing through his body. There was a flurry of slapping sounds as the monster darted down the corridor toward him, its paws using the walls for leverage as it propelled itself toward its prey.

Now would have been a smart time to light a goddamn match, Lang thought to himself. But when he blinked, he realized that he could make out a deep shadow within the black, not five feet away from him. He lunged forward, ducking down and making an upward sweep with the blade. It punctured something; his arm jolted, the hilt digging into his palm. The Eagle screamed and flailed, kicking and scratching at the walls. Dust peppered Lang's cheeks, landed on his tongue when he gasped for air and left his mouth tasting of chalk.

He withdrew the blade and staggered backwards. The creature fell still.

Trembling but buzzed from the kill, Lang slipped the matches from his pocket and struck one. His eyes stung and flooded with tears, already accustomed to the pitch darkness of the cave. He blinked away the sting and looked down at the Eagle. The knife had pretty much gutted it, black innards spilling out under the lifeless carcass. Gold flecks glimmered in the matchlight. An open gunshot wound festered on the monster's shoulder, flinging his mind back to the assault on the convoy that morning and the creature that had escaped.

Lang let out a snort. "I knew I'd see you again, you old fuck."

There was a cackling sound up ahead, echoing through the cavern from somewhere further down the narrow pathway.

He blew out the match.

Lang kept the Green River in his hand as he picked his way over the carcass. It was slimy underfoot, his boots slipping down over the toad-like flesh. He dug his elbows into the walls for purchase and clambered as gracefully as he could over the dead Fallen Eagle.

There were more of the monsters a short way ahead of him. He could sense it. He didn't want to be stuck like a pig in a barrel when twenty of the beasts came through the tunnel. He steeled himself and broke into a trot, hoping there wasn't a sudden drop in the cavern floor along the way. His footfalls echoed a little, but the impacted rock seemed to absorb most of the sound. He hurried along, trying to remember to breathe, senses on high alert. He frowned when a gentle breeze sent a chill across his cheeks.

The air up until that point had been warm and stale. He stopped and reached out, his palms smoothing over the rough canyon walls. His fingers groped around a sharp right curve in the tunnel's pathway. The cool air washed over his fingertips, and he felt his heart rate speed up. The chamber. The old man had told him to find the chamber. Find the king.

Trying hard to keep the tremor from his fingers, Lang slipped the candle from his back pocket and reached again for his matchbox. The tiny sticks slid together as he lifted the box out, the faint noise in the quiet like a barn being razed by dynamite rather than the shifting of a few dozen matches. He tensed.

The sound of shuffling came from a distant place.

He followed the pathway on its curve to the right, the cool air now sending the hairs on his arms standing up. A foul stench hit his nostrils. He edged forward, both the smell and his fear increasing with each step.

He stopped when he sensed that the surroundings had changed. Instead of the instinctive claustrophobia of the narrow hallway in the canyon, he suddenly felt exposed to the elements, the cold rushing around him from all sides. He stepped back quickly, planting his back flat against the wall, and hoped he hadn't been seen.

There was the sound of padding footsteps, but none

of them seemed to be advancing upon him. Instead, the Eagles appeared to be occupied with other tasks. There was a weird sound coming from the open room, a strange sucking noise that was occasionally punctuated by a loud snort. He was used to the creatures shrieking in battle, but these—however many there were—were unusually quiet.

Well, buddy, Lang thought to himself. *It's now or never. You've had a good run of it. Let's just see what today's gonna bring.*

He struck one of the matches against his thigh and brought the flame to the candle wick.

When he was sure the flame had taken, he stuck the wax stick into the ground, wedged in a crevasse of rock. He stepped into the chamber as a cacophony of shrieks sounded all around him.

For a second, Langston just blinked at what he was seeing. The candle gave a small portion of the room a gentle amber glow, but the room was huge, its walls undulating with moving black bodies that glimmered with gold. At the highest point of the cavern, moonlight spilled in through a small break in the rock. It shone a beam of silver onto a dark grey blob that clung to the side of the mountain. It was a Fallen Eagle, but at the same time it wasn't. Its limbs seemed to merge into the mountain itself, molten gold connecting one to the other. Its features were like the smaller Eagles—its lithe, dog-like body undulating with greyish flesh. But its face was markedly different. A row of blinking eyes crowned its head like a halo and, judging from its position slapped flat against the wall, Lang guessed that was how it saw everything. A mouth, if it could even be called that, split open down its back. The orifice contained a spiral of pinprick teeth stuck messily into black gums. It let out a scream, a call to arms, that made every Fallen Eagle whip its attention toward Lang standing small in the chamber's entrance.

This was the Golden King, Lang knew. How in the Sam Hill was he going to kill it?

He yanked his Whitworth from the holster across his back and began to fire. Making a noise wasn't an issue anymore and, even if the shots caused a rockslide, perhaps that would be better. Easier than facing the monumental task ahead of him.

The Fallen Eagles leapt from the walls, advancing on him like giant rats. He took aim at what he knew to be the most effective targets, the soft bit of the head, all the while driving forward. The trigger finally gave a dull click, and he threw the Whitworth to the side. Lang slashed wildly with the Green River as he plunged his left hand into his side holster and drew his revolver. It felt lighter in his hand than the rifle, and he sent out seven of the nine available shots before he'd even drawn a second breath. The seventh bullet punched through two of the creatures at once, and one of them tumbled to the side, catching its nearest team-mate off guard. The advancing monster stumbled over the body, and Lang took his chance to get closer to the king. He darted forward, scrambling over the mass of death. As he leaped over the creature that had tripped, he drove his knife down with his left hand, skewering it straight through the top of the head. It slumped down on top of the Eagle that had caused it to fall.

The eighth and ninth bullets tore through the guards

that had been crouching directly below the king. Langston tossed the empty gun and took his trusty Green River into his dominant hand. It was no longer a secondary weapon. It was all he had left. But, somehow, he'd made it to the canyon wall. The king was positioned about ten feet above him, the beast's grunts rising over the sound of the screaming soldiers that were coming for Lang. There was no time.

He dug deep and found a final burst of strength, hauling himself up the rocks. He felt the hot breath of one of the Fallen Eagles scampering up behind him, heard the thundering paws closing in on him. He just needed to finish the king before they took him out. This was his one chance.

Pushing his toes flat against the rock face and driving the knife hilt into a crevasse to brace himself, he swung his free hand up and grasped a hunk of flesh on the king's back. It let out a grunt that sounded like a confused fart, the back end of the sound squeaking upwards in tone. He dug his fingertips into the pulsating flesh and arched his other arm, the blade catching the moonlight.

The back of his hand whacked an overhang of rock.

Reflexively, his fingers shot open at the shock of the blow.

The knife skittered down the rockface.

Langston let out a wail of desperation.

He was shit out of luck. Within seconds, the creatures would be on him. He thought of the old man. He was an idiot to have believed the rantings of the crazy old fool. *Save the whole dang country. The gift.* What a crazy fucker.

The old man's words sounded again, pushing through

the terrified fuzz of Lang's thoughts. The hand that wasn't wrist deep in monster flesh groped at his chest. His fingers wrapped around the ornamental obsidian blade, gifted to him by an Arikara warrior for helping his people through flash flood waters.

A four-pronged ice pick drove into Lang's calf, the hooked claws of one of the creatures. The Eagle's grip tightened in his muscle, the beast making ready to fling Langston off its king, the other creatures swarming, snarling and snapping below.

Lang snapped the cord of the necklace and plunged the stone blade into the king's side, but the flesh resisted, as though he were trying to cut a cactus with a spoon. The swing of his body meant that the leg that wasn't being clutched by the Eagle pressed into the rock, and he felt something wedged in his boot.

Harlan's blade.

Almost twisting in two, Lang leaned down and snatched the handle. He jerked his arm up and stabbed at the king, then forced the stone necklace in next to the blade, deep into the gaping wound a moment before the Fallen Eagle yanked him down and away from the creature attached to the rockface.

The movement ripped the sharp flint into the toadish flesh, tearing downwards through grey mush and liquid gold.

As Lang fell, he found satisfaction in the sound the king made. Another fart-like expulsion of breath. This one, a mournful sigh of defeat.

A pulse tore through the mountain and Lang had to cover his ears rather than attempt to break his fall. He hit the bed of the canyon heavy, the breath coursing out of him. Winded and weapon less, he looked helplessly up at the monsters that advanced on him, poised to kill him.

Instead, the strange air that rushed out of the dying king's body hit the swarm full force, flinging them back against the walls of the canyon. Screaming and squealing, the creatures kicked and flailed as the rock absorbed them, sucking their flesh into the wall and making it solid, gold flecks bursting from the evaporated monsters and fluttering down through the moonlit cavern like sudden rainfall on a clear summer night.

Lang watched the sparkles fall around him, gradually catching his breath. It made him think of Harlan, and he sent a thank you up to the boy's spirit for leaving him with a second knife. Above him, the dead king slowly descended into the rockface, the molten gold solidifying and falling in heavy nuggets. Just pocketing one of the pebbles would make Lang the richest man in the US. Only, gold was worthless when he was trapped inside a mountain.

After a while, Lang sat up and set about fixing his leg, wrapping a piece of torn shirt around the gaping wounds.

A few hours later, the candle went out.

Later, he wasn't sure how long, he figured he'd need to try and find a way out. He hobbled through the endless black corridors, occasionally striking a match but seeing nothing but cavern walls.

There was no hunger or thirst in the canyon, but still time struck out endlessly.

He took each day as it came, and each day was the same. Darkness and walls surrounding him, whichever way he turned.

When he'd searched every inch of the inside of the mountain, what felt like months or years later, he found his way back into the open room of the king's lair. Now, sunlight cut gently through the opening above him.

Lang rested back against the cavern wall beside the pile of gold nuggets and wrapped his arms around his knees, rocking slightly. He looked at his gnarled and veiny hands and didn't recognise them as his own.

He began to sing.

Days later he heard the voices of long-forgotten friends and followed the sound out into the sunlight.

Monastery Blood Moon

Act 1. Spilled Chardonnay

A buzz ripples through the small crowd of art buyers and influencers that mingle near the installation of mirrors. The blood moon is rising, and soon the largest mirror will catch the pale pink burst of its eerie glow. Artist Bara Varey has painstakingly set up a hundred panes of glass, each mathematically calculated and angled so the uppermost circular disc will send a cascade of pinkish light spiralling down to the ground. The old monastery on the hill is the perfect setting for such a bold attempt at modern art. Its huge round window set with slivers of age-faded stained glass already casts sheens of gentle colour across the scuffed oak flooring. Dust from the old timbers shimmer in the atmosphere above the lucky ticketholders who have first dibs to see Varey's latest artistic masterpiece.

The promoter mills about the group, a monocle clenched between the apple of his left cheek and his neatly sculpted eyebrow. I watch him glide over to a woman wearing a huge necklace that takes up most of her chest. The large, polished stones shake as she leans up to accept the air kisses he drops close to each cheekbone, and he clasps both her hand and that of the woman standing next to her, an older lady whose platinum hair is teased and blown into an alarming '60s beehive style. A bored-looking waiter slouches as he carries a silver tray through the small throng, stopping when Bara's protégé, a fresh-faced young artist with paint streaks marking her fingers and the tips of her wild brown curls, sneaks two flutes of champagne from the tray and downs them, replacing the empty glasses and taking a third. She and the waiter smile conspiratorially and glance around to make sure nobody else has noticed. The waiter almost runs into a portly middle-aged man whose neck is swathed in a thick blue scarf, and the man barks a reprimand before angrily snatching a flute for himself. *What an ass*, I think, wondering how he can stand to wear an itchy woollen scarf indoors in summer. I grin to myself when the young artist catches the waiter's eye and flips scarf-guy the bird behind his back, instantly turning the waiter's frown upside down.

So far, the waiter and paint-hair girl are the only people who seem remotely tolerable. We are way out of our depth.

Us? We're just the band. We stand on the stage and try to ignore the raised eyebrows shot our way by the immaculately turned-out gallery owners and influencers who wave tiny hors d'oeuvres in one hand and fragile flutes of champagne in the other. We don't fit in, but that's okay. Tonight, we aren't Piss on a Gremlin, pioneers of melodic pop-punk interspersed with a little operatic vibrato (trust me, it sounds great, once you get used to it). Tonight only, we have a tamed-down sound as a favour to our drummer's uncle. He runs a local event management company and begged us to perform when the snooty string ensemble they'd originally hired for the *Monastery Moon* event dropped out at the last minute.

We've tried to scrub up, but there's no denying that we belong in our usual sleazy rock club, with its walls and tattered upholstery permeated with the lingering scent of stale beer and decades-old cigarette smoke. This is another world. I stare up at the towering wood-panelled walls, the crosshatch of timbers above us making up the ancient rafters. Most of the mirrors are slender rectangles, a hundred of them spiralling down from the huge circle that makes up the centrepiece. I see myself reflected back in the lower sections. Tonight, I'm not Tidy Angela, singer and guitarist of Piss on a Gremlin. Tonight, I'm just plain old Angela. It sucks.

Mal shook his head when he first saw the artist's set-up. "That's how you open a spirit gate," the drummer said, matter-of-factly.

Sally smirked, looking up from tuning her bass. "How's that, now?"

"Setting up mirrors to reflect each other. That's how spirits can come through. I saw it on Ghost Hunt Hunks."

"Everybody knows you don't watch that show for the ghosts. Or the hunting, for that matter."

I'd grinned at Sally's observation, but took a moment under the gently swaying mirrors, feeling small. If there was ever a place for spirits to come through, the decaying monastery on the hill under the cast of a blood moon would be a good place to start.

Now, I'm just keen to start playing. The blood moon is due at any moment, and the pretentious gang waiting under the ambitious installation who've paid an extortionate ticket price will have our guts if we aren't playing music when the moon's light hits the first mirror.

I glance back at the others and return their nods. I almost do a double-take at our strange appearance. Gone are the tattered battle jackets and fishnets. Sally's usually spiky red hair is combed back and pinned neatly behind her ears. Instead of black-rimmed eyes, she has brushed a little brown powder over the lids. Mal looks years younger, wearing a white shirt and tie instead of his usual T-shirt, a safety-pinned homage to Vivienne Westwood. We don't look like ourselves. But we are ready.

Almost. Bara Varey has fixed me with a hawkish stare, and I realise there's no way I can introduce ourselves as Piss on a Gremlin. Not unless we want to piss away our chance of getting paid for the night. I need a new name, and fast.

As much as I'd like to do it just for the laugh, I am a little scared of this crazy artist and the simmering rage that flares behind her tear-drop-shaped spectacles. When we were unloading the van earlier, I accidentally stepped too close to one of the mirrors when I was reversing in with my Marshall amp. From the aggressive half-squeal, half growl, and the sudden rush of a dark shape throwing itself between me and the glass, I thought I was being attacked by a sasquatch. But nope. It was Bara in her swishing kaftan, a glass of white wine held accusingly out toward me.

"Do be careful, you... oafs!" she snapped, checking her precious mirrors. Then her attention fell to the dark stain streaking her chest. She scowled up at me and swiped a hand at the splash of wine, tutting loudly. "Ugh, you bitch.... You made me spill my chardonnay!"

I clear my throat, lean into the microphone, and look directly at Bara. "Good evening, ladies and gentlemen. We are Spilled Chardonnay. Enjoy the installation."

Act 2. The Installation

We've decided on a few covers. Crowd pleasers from the Eurythmics, Billy Joel, and The Eagles. We aren't used to playing this slowly, and every so often Mal's beat speeds up, Sally's hands trip faster over the bassline, and I fight to slow us down. My guitar feels a little alien in my hands as I pick out a melody.

We get through the first couple of songs, my voice getting bolder the more time passes. These people beneath us make me nervous. Not a mosh-pit in sight.

In fact, they barely react to the music at all. They are enthralled by the mirrors, even if there is nothing to see. The paltry splashes of champagne in their flutes are yet to be drunk. Some crumbs of the miniscule hors d'oeuvres still perch between thumb and forefinger. If we were at the battle of the bands, the crowd would be well into its sixth round of drinks by now, thoughts of kebabs and burgers on the way home popping into the minds of the rowdy gang of rockers.

One head nods along in the crowd, and I catch the

eye of a familiar man who seems a little awkward and out of place here. He's tall and broad, with a cool angled fade haircut topped with neat afro curls. Beneath his tailored brown suit worn over a silky blue T-shirt, I see the tell-tale lumps and bumps of well-defined muscle. While I try my hardest not to break into a Bad Religion cover for our third song, I remember that he has been to some of our gigs. He is usually accompanied by his girlfriend, who sports a stunning blaze of fire-red hair and a horseshoe septum piercing. I scan the crowd but see no sign of her, and I'm a little disappointed. She's always one of our most enthusiastic audience members. I guess she'd rather chop off her arm than appear at something as sedate as this event, and that her partner must have a job that requires him to be there out of necessity rather than choice. I'd say hi after the installation is over, but from the way he's frowning at us in puzzlement as he tries to sway to the music, I'm guessing he has been unable to place Spilled Chardonnay.

A wiry man wearing a grey checked suit at least a size too small for him sidles over and says something about the mirrors. Nodding, fade haircut follows his gaze to stare up at the installation.

Then it happens. We are halfway through a gentle rendition of *Sweet Dreams (Are Made of This)* when the monastery plunges into a peculiar dusky darkness. We all cast our eyes to the large circular mirror suspended in the rafters. Pink light streaks across its glistening pane.

Even over our music, I hear oooh's and ahhhh's from the crowd. Thirteen eager faces tilt upwards to watch the spectacle.

It's beautiful, I'll give the artist that. The pink shimmer gives the upmost mirror the illusion of being suddenly solid, and from my vantage point on the stage I can't see anything else reflected in its pane but the light of the strange moon. Then, like rain trickling down through a jungle canopy of leaves, each of the descending mirrors picks up a sliver of the light and casts it onto the next immaculately angled pane below it. It spirals down, only taking a couple of seconds for each sheet of glass to catch the pink, but the effect really is something.

And then something climbs through the circular mirror.

The onlookers gasp, awed at the mirage of a creature clambering out through the pane. The promoter with the pretentious monocle turns to the artist, open-mouthed. "However did you do it?" he guffaws.

"I... I didn't!" The fear on Bara Varey's face causes my fingers to freeze on my guitar strings. She takes three quick steps backwards, staring up in horror.

The creature wraps its hands around the edge of the mirror and climbs onto the rim, sending the mirror swinging from side to side, the installation ruined. Purple, yellow, and blue smears of light dance around the walls as it reflects the huge stained-glass disc above the door instead of the moonlight. But whatever it was about the blood moon that opened the door to allow the creature to climb through is still in effect, because a second grotesque face peeks out of the centre of the pane of glass.

The first monster perches on the swinging circle and peers down at the gathering. It is roughly the size of a Dalmatian, but its face is more simian. It reminds me of the macaques at the local zoo, but it is completely hairless, its flesh the sludgy green-brown of Dickensian prison slop.

Oh, and it also has wings.

It unfurls them, its wingspan a metre or so, the flesh between the prongs of its tendons almost transparent.

We have all stopped playing, a rumbling final note from Sally's bass echoing out through the monastery. Before the note's reverberations end, another creature has crawled out of the mirror.

There is still confusion in the small crowd huddled under the monsters. Those who haven't seen the artist's horrified reaction are still uncertain whether this is part of the show. A feat of genius illusionary magic that they never expected to see in the small town's long-abandoned monastery.

A tiny woman in a patchwork cape scurries like a brightly coloured beetle over to Bara and whispers urgently to her. When Bara shakes her head, the woman holds up her arms under the canopy, reminding me of Joseph and the Technicolor Dreamcoat. "Everybody, calmly make your way to the main doors. This is not a part of the installation."

Too-tight suit looks at her with a sneer. "Oh, very good, Patricia. Is it Hallowe'en already? I don't believe it for a second!"

"Who do you think I've got up there?" Bara snaps, hysteria creeping into her voice. "My nephews in costumes?!"

With that, she bolts for the heavy front doors.

It's a mistake.

The largest of the monsters lets out a shriek that

makes my heart sink to the floor. One of the smaller creatures (which looks eerily like one of the stone gargoyles that sit on the edges of the Monastery's roof) peers down with beady eyes and sees the moving target. It drops like a stone through the air until its wings pillow out at its sides. Its body lifts into an elegant curve. It clamps its talons into Bara's slender back and pumps its wings three times, hovering on the spot with the artist suspended a couple of feet off the ground. The monster's jaws open to reveal long, pointed snake fangs. It sinks them into her neck and chomps. Blood geysers out, the once-pink panes now reflecting spurts of shocking crimson.

There is instant chaos.

Champagne flutes smash. The last of the hors-d'oeuvres tumble to the floor and are smushed underfoot as the attendees scramble to find cover.

The big boss monster makes a grab for Patricia, drawn to her brightly coloured cape. For a moment, she looks like an umbrella with two chunky legs wiggling underneath a canopy of jewel reds, yellows, and blues. Then, she slips out of the cloak and lands in a neat crouch, looking different in her all-black underclothes. Momentarily stunned, she clambers to her feet and makes a beeline for the huge statue of the archangel Gabriel that stands off to the side of the main hall. The largest of the creatures is tangled in the thick woven fabric of the cape, confused at his suddenly lightened load. He wheels around in the air, kicking his hands and feet to rid himself of the cloth trap.

Four or five of the crowd have found places to hide. Too-small suit, huge necklace lady, and beehive have rolled underneath rows of seating. I can see beehive woman holding her nose in the shadows under the benches, trying not to sneeze as she lies in a pile of disturbed dust forty years in the making. Fade haircut has managed to shelter behind the speaker boxes at the back of the room, and I watch as he casually side-steps away towards the kitchen in the back. I'd follow him if I could. The kitchen is small, used occasionally for the Christmas soup kitchen and for caterers to prep their tiny morsels of posh event food, but my mind lingers on what might be stored in its drawers and cupboards. Knives. Cleavers. Plenty of sharp things better suited to a monster attack than a guitar and a microphone.

Meanwhile, the smaller creatures pick off the stragglers. The young artist with paint flecks in her curls screams as she is pinned to the ground. A monster clasps her ribcage in its talons and squeezes. Blood spurts from her mouth as her chest crunches and bones snap into organs. The waiter is lifted up by the ankle, his other leg dangling painfully as the creature flies higher. Halfway to the rafters, another of the monsters glides past, its claw swiping out like a cat sleepily batting a passing fly. A shower of blood, eviscerated organs, and piss scatter down onto the people below, and the gargoyle drops the waiter. His body lands on the monocled promoter, who was backing away from one of the monsters. Another gargoyle hops forward, vulture-like, takes the promoter's head in both front paws, twists sharply, and pulls it off. The monocle bounces across the floor like a tossed coin.

Something grabs my arm, and I am frozen in terror, until Sally whispers sharply next to my ear, "Come on,

Tidy, for fuck's sake!"

Stiff-limbed, I turn and see Mal peeking out from behind the drum kit. There is a gulley behind the stage, and he is crouched in it. It's not the perfect hiding place, but it will do.

Act 3. Riot at the Party Portal

I follow Sally, creeping quickly along the stage with my left hand clamped around my guitar neck. I'm still clutching my wireless microphone in the other hand, so I stuff it in my back pocket, freeing up one arm so I can clamber down into the pit.

I'm about to lower myself down when something yanks me back and my guitar smashes against my hip. I realise the guitar cord is still attached to the amp, and I am literally at the end of my rope. *Idiot*, I think as I take the input carefully in my right hand and twist it.

Three blasts of staccato static ring out through the amp.

Of course.

Why am I such a fucking—

I can't finish the thought, because daggers are plugging into my back and upper arm. And then I see myself, wild-eyed and desperate, reflected in pane after pane of mirrored glass as the gargoyle lifts me higher and higher into the air. The monster is unreal, its flesh puckered and scaled like an iguana, the stench of burning hair coming from its body.

Sulphur, I think. *Oh, fuck. Does that mean...*

A sudden noise explodes in the air. It sounds like the

most wretchedly beautiful power-chord ever created. That's exactly what it is, I realise. Glancing down at the stage, I see Sally shredding on her Spector bass, using the side of her pick and scraping it against the strings. Mal is to the side of her, angling his amp in my direction with all the nobs turned up as far as they'll go. Shocked, the beast lets go of me. I fall through the air, hurtling toward one of the roof beams.

Oh shit. This isn't good...

My guitar takes the brunt of the fall, the neck splintering in two in my hands. The impact knocks the air from my lungs, and all I can do is lie on the trashed guitar and fight to draw breath. There is pain blooming in my thigh; I can feel it when I wrap my legs tighter around the beam. And my left forearm has three fairly deep slashes from the creature's claws.

But I'm alive.

I peer down at the ground below me. Sally and Mal have disappeared behind the stage, and I can't see any creatures homing in on them. Cape-less Patricia is being picked at by two of the creatures. In a feat of insane strength, she somehow manages to topple the archangel Gabriel statue, squashing one of the gargoyles. But the act of defiance only spurs the other monsters on, and Patricia vanishes under a swarm of green wings.

Across the room, the row of benches is being flanked, and beehive is dragged from her hiding place, leaving tracks in the thick dust. She lets out a half-sneeze, half cry, before her throat is clawed out and she is forever silenced.

Wobbling, keeping my hurt leg pressed firmly against the hard rafter, I struggle into a precarious sitting position. I lament the fact that my beloved Epiphone SG is in pieces. But at least I now have some form of defence the next time one of them swoops at me.

I'm in a cluster of rafters that spindle out from an alcove, three buttresses with a criss-cross network of ancient beams giving support to the lower ceiling. The wood here is positioned slightly behind another strong support bolster that angles upward, making a sharp right angle in front of me. I wedge the body of my guitar into the V shape, the curve of polished blue wood to the left of the neck joint jamming into the splintered timber. I give it a few sharp tugs. It doesn't budge.

Reaching down, I follow the trail of strings to retrieve the snapped neck, groping until I have the headstock in my hand, the nubs of the tuning nuts cold against my skin. I reverse along the beam a little, shakily reaching up until I can hook the fractured neck behind the adjacent V of the wooden support. Releasing all but one of the strings so they hang loose, I wedge it into position, again testing its weight. The string is taut, stretching across the front of my face. I'm hoping that the light bouncing off the mirrors will act as a kind of mirage.

One of the smaller gargoyles finishes feasting on the neck of the man with the thick woollen scarf. The monster rears back and catches sight of me perched in the rafters. Then it makes an alarming beeline straight for me.

I quickly position myself behind the E-string tripwire and brace myself. At the last moment, just as the creature opens its mouth, I shuffle to the side, trying hard not to lose my balance. There is a strange, dull pinging sound as the guitar string sears into both corners of the creature's mouth, then slices through its throat. Its body trembles and tips downward, and the guitar string twangs again as flesh tears away. The gargoyle spins as it drops through the air, leaving behind a chunk of greenish gum stuck to my E-string.

I glance down at the stage and see my friends fighting the creatures with their own instruments. Mal is swinging his hi-hat stand like a metal club, bashing one of the monsters until it lies in a crumpled heap on the stage. Sally is destroying one of them with her bass, striking the creature in the head repeatedly until there is a dark puddle of blood and brain matter.

But for every monster we kill, two more appear through the portal. I am helpless, stuck on the beam. There is no way for me to get down without killing myself, and I don't have anything to effectively throw at the mirror to smash it.

"Mal!" I yell. "Throw your cymbals at the mirrors!"

My shouting attracts one of the newest arrivals to the portal party. This eager gargoyle launches at me from above and speeds up as it approaches. The tripwire snares it across the palm, searing through two of its clawed fingers. The wire stops the attack, but the string gives one long *ping* and finally breaks.

Mal has understood the assignment, at least, and begins to unscrew the high-hat clutch to release the shiny brass cymbals. Behind him, one of the gargoyles crawls up onto the stage, almost out of sight behind the drums.

"Look out!" I scream.

There's no chance Mal can move in time. He's engaged in unscrewing the cymbals. Sally is in a battle of her own as she kneels on one of the creatures, the neck of her bass clamped over the monster's throat, her arms trembling with effort. Mal is on his own.

At least, that is until fade haircut leaps up from the side of the stage with a mini blowtorch in his hand. I remember the caterers using it as we were led through the tiny kitchen when we first arrived, blasting the tops of the tiny crème brûlée bites. He could have made an easy getaway through the back exit, but instead chose to help us. He jabs fire into the creature's face and it goes up in an inferno.

Mal wastes no time and releases the cymbal from its mooring while fade haircut sprints across and kneels beside the gargoyle struggling under Sally's weight. I didn't see it before, but he also has a large kitchen knife, and he plunges the blade straight through the creature's head, then helps Sally to her feet.

Mal holds the cymbal in his hand, gauging the distance between him and the mirror. He winds up and throws it. It has the height, but not the aim. The drummer swipes his hand through his hair, defeated. He looks uncertainly at the second cymbal.

"Just do it, Mal!" I yell.

He looks up at me with a fleeting expression of helplessness, before his jaw sets in steely determination. He wraps his fingertips around the edge of the cymbal, its length resting against his forearm, then grunts and launches the second cymbal from his hand. It shimmers as it travels upwards. When it reaches the uppermost heights of the installation, it begins to curve with bowling ball precision.

The cymbal makes a vibrating hum when it collides

with the central mirror, shattering through its middle with an ear-splitting crash. Shards of glass begin to fall and, in a chain reaction, the slivers tumble into the sheets below them, splintering pane after pane of mirrored glass. It's like a crystal chandelier forming in mid-air, the pieces of mirror still reflecting the pinkish sky and the beams of the stage lighting.

There is pandemonium from the creatures. The large boss monster screams, and I fight to keep my hands where they are—trembling against the beam and not clasping my ears to instinctively cover them. The monster swoops down from its perch, seeking the portal mirror that is nothing but a wire frame swinging softly from side to side. The cymbal sticks out just behind it, clasped neatly between two of the old roof beams. I watch the monster begin to make its biggest mistake, and suddenly I know that I might be able to save myself.

The gargoyle swoops under the cascade of falling glass, disappearing within the shimmering column for a second. Moments later, its squeal and the sound of frantic flapping can be heard over the endless chinks of shattering mirror. It bursts through the tumbling shards, its dark blood pattering in a steady stream from countless wounds on its strange green body. Its wings are in tatters and, like the circular mirror that once crowned the installation, all that remains is the slender coat-hanger-thin wires of its tendons.

A stalling aircraft, it begins to fall into a tailspin, pattering fountains of blood. And since my trap is no longer effective, it takes me down with it.

As we spin, I wrap my arms around its body. My weight stops its uncontrollable spinning, and I am face-to-face with the creature. Its eyes are cold and bloodthirsty, and its mouth opens, showing a forked tongue and four long fangs. Its neck retracts, ready to strike.

I flinch, but just before it makes its attack we hit the ground, my forehead slamming into its strange leathery snout in a perfect Glasgow kiss. My body is sprawled on top of the creature, cushioning my fall although the shudder of the impact wracks my lungs and sends shockwaves through my spine. There is glass everywhere from the mirrors smashed above, and my arms are cut to ribbons.

I try to stand, but the creature grabs my ankle, holds me close while its head rears back to strike with those deadly fangs. Its nose is streaming translucent green slime from where I headbutted it, and it snorts and sputters, giving me a moment to counterattack. Without thinking, I pluck the microphone from my back pocket and slam it down its wide throat. The silver housing of the mic tears through the back of its oesophagus and the bulbous honeycomb of the mic's cap sticks up in its gaping mouth like a tasteless, music-themed Hallowe'en Jack-o'-lantern. The creature shudders once more, pisses itself, and then finally chokes to death in a pool of green blood.

I limp to my feet and look around at the monastery, in shock.

Too-small suit was directly under the mirrors when the cymbal hit, having fled from the rows of benches when beehive was snagged by the gargoyles. Seared chunks of him lie in a puddle to my left. Now, his suit is too big.

Okay, so I didn't exactly like these people, but I'm not a monster. I shed a tear for too-small suit, beehive, and all the other pretentious somebodies who lie dead on the monastery floor. It was a massacre.

But the portal is closed. We may just make it out of here, as long as I don't bleed out. The cuts don't hurt too badly. Not yet. But that's because they're deep. I didn't land in a pile of confetti, and these aren't papercuts.

I watch as Sally, fade hair, and Mal pick off the remaining few creatures, surrounding me to fight to the last breath. The loss of the portal seems to have weakened the beasts. A quick blast of the catering torch followed by a slap from Sally's bass and a finishing blow of Mal's drumstick wipes out the last of them.

It's over.

Act 4. Encore

Sally patches me up as best as she can. I don't want to stay in the monastery a moment longer than I have to, so we hobble outside to try and get a phone signal.

Apart from the band, fade hair—who introduces himself as Leon—is the only other survivor. In the moonlight, he peers at me curiously, then snaps his fingers. "Piss on a Gremlin."

I give him a small smile. "You're damn right. I don't think Spilled Chardonnay will be making it for a comeback tour."

Sally, her call to emergency services made successfully, lowers her phone and rolls her eyes. "Thank fuck for that."

"Never again," Mal agrees, swiping his drumstick across his jeans, leaving a streak of green gargoyle blood. "Hey, maybe we should change our name to Piss on a Gargoyle."

A swanky car pulls up as I lower myself to a seat on the monastery steps, gritting my teeth when the split flesh on the backs of my legs presses against the makeshift bandages. A dapper looking gent hops out of the car, his blond hair slicked back so severely, I think for a second in the near darkness that he's bald.

He looks us over, delight blooming on his face. He claps his hands and rocks on his toes excitedly. "Is this part of the exhibit? Wow! I didn't realise there was am-dram theatre as well. I was worried I'd missed it all. Well, come on!"

He skips up the steps and pushes open the heavy door, then looks back at us with an entitled frown.

"I've paid for my ticket, after all. Can't you give me an encore?"

A gargoyle that must have been waiting in the rafters rushes him, digging its talons into his chest. It lifts him straight up into the air and flies away, the man's screams echoing around the trees.

"Encore," I say, and give my best thespian bow to the speck disappearing into the fading pink light. I might feel bad for the guy, regardless of his rudeness, but I've lost about two pints of blood and so my tolerance is low.

I watch the silhouette of them both against the full moon.

"Uhhh...Tidy?" Mal stammers.

I follow his bewildered gaze to the huge stained-glass window above the door, where a greenish-grey arm is somehow groping out of the pane of glass. Seconds later, a snout pokes out. It snarls and pants, struggling to squeeze itself through whatever remnant of the portal is lingering in the ancient panes.

"We have to break the windows," Sally yells.

I shrug, the effects of the blood loss making me apathetic to everything. Since I'm sitting directly underneath the windows, Leon scoops an arm under my pits and helps me to stagger a couple of metres away. He puts me down and turns back to Sally, eager to help us. I feel as though Leon is now part of the crew. A roadie for life, whether he likes it or not. He hunts on the grass for a stone, finding a chunk of old and worn granite. He rears back and pitches and the hunk of rock hurtles through the stained glass, closing the new portal and sending the shorn off arm and snout of the creature tumbling to the entrance steps. The arm lands heavily on the step where I was just sitting, green blood mingling with my own.

Although his effort has been triumphant, Leon peers back at me with a pensive look on his face. "I think we need to break all of the windows, just in case the portal can open inside them all. We need to find more stones..."

Sally gives a whistle, off to the side, my spare Epiphone slung over her shoulders. Mal is beside her, the extension cord from inside the monastery held in his hands. An over-crammed multi-plug stuffed with connections that lead to our huge amp that Bara Varey told us in no uncertain terms not to bring into the monastery for fear of it shattering her precious mirrors is sticking up from the extension. "We have a better idea," Sally beams.

She gives Mal the nod, and he swipes a hand over the

volume and tone dials, turning them all up to the max.

"Wait!" I call. Clinging onto Leon for support, I hobble over to Sally and hold out my hands. She passes me my old Epiphone, the one I used when I was a student. It's covered in stickers and dents and it feels like home in my hands.

Sally grins when Mal plugs her bass into the socket and holds it out to her. This will be our finest duet.

"I've always wanted to do this," I say, and thrash out the meanest, loudest chord I've ever played in my life, Sally's bass joining me with a tone so powerful it feels like the ground beneath us is rumbling. Birds and bats scatter from the trees around us. As though curious to see where its portal friends might be, the rogue gargoyle who flew away with the latecomer circles overhead. The windows hold fast for a second, and I wonder if Bara may have been wrong. If we could have rocked the joint with our chunky Fender Stage amp without causing any damage after all.

But suddenly the sound of shattering pierces the air and the beautiful coloured glass splinters into fragments that patter down onto the stone steps. The gargoyle flying above us gives a squark of despair and drops like a shot duck, landing within arm's reach of me.

I'm in pain but blasting out a screaming power chord loud enough to explode a bunch of windows has certainly put a pep in my step. I shrug the strap from my shoulders and hold my first guitar by its neck. With a grunt, I swing it down with all my might and cave the gargoyle's head in with the wooden body. Green blood spatters across my collection of skate and band stickers and, to my relief, the neck doesn't break.

Mal nods at me. I hear a *ziiiip* sound and look down where his fingers are tugging down the zip of his dress pants. He lets out a huge sigh and begins to piss on the gargoyle.

Big Gulps and Bigfoot

Gross! Get your filthy big foot off my dash," Jean scolded her sister. Geri had insisted on walking through the convenience store at the rest stop in bare feet, and Jean cringed at the thought of what her soles were now transferring onto her car's interior.

"It's not doing any harm," Geri said, wiggling her grubby toes.

"It's distracting me. It stinks. Plus, haven't you seen the X-rays of people who had their feet up when they crashed?"

The foot stilled and Jean felt her sister's eyes boring into her. "No. What happens?"

"Their thighbone ends up through their hip."

"Bullshit."

"It's true. If I crash this thing and you become a human pretzel, don't come crying to me."

Geri lifted the foot and set it down on the mat. She shifted in her seat, crossing and uncrossing her legs. Jean knew that could only mean one thing, and she tried to ignore the irritation that built up in her at knowing they'd been at a rest stop just fifteen minutes ago and were currently hours from the next one.

"I need to pee," Geri blurted, eyeing up the empty Big Gulp cup she'd just guzzled as though she was considering whether it would double as a makeshift porta-potty.

"I told you to go at the rest stop," Jean told her sister, trying to keep the clipped annoyance out of her words.

"I didn't need to go, then."

"Maybe you shouldn't have got a drink the size of your head in that case." The siblings had been on the road for two and a half days now, and Jean couldn't wait until they reached their destination and could separate for a while. She loved her sister, but fuck, she could be annoying.

Now, Geri wiggled in her seat, plucking her jean shorts away from her waist to relieve the pressure. She moaned. "I'm literally about to piss my pants, here."

"Do you want me to pull over?" Jean knew the answer—another reason why her anger was growing.

"I'm not going in the grass like an animal."

Jean sighed. "Well, you're not going in my car."

Folding her arms, Geri scowled. "I'll just go in the cup, then toss it out the window. What's wrong with that?"

"Are you out of your mind? First off, I don't want to see your bare ass sticking up from the footwell whenever I need to check my mirror, I don't want your piss spilling out all over my car, and you are not throwing trash filled with piss out of my window! It's disgusting." Jean had turned to look at Geri with incredulous rage, setting her eyes back on the road in time to turn a corner. "Shit!"

She slammed on the brake, swerving gently onto

the grassy embankment to avoid the two cars that had stopped in the middle of the road.

Geri screamed, clamping both hands over her groin to hold in her pee as the seatbelt jerked across her middle. "Fuck!"

"Are you okay?" Jean gasped, the build-up of older sibling fury evaporating with the shock and relief of avoiding the accident.

"No! I almost wet my pants!" Geri yelled, furious. She tugged the door handle and kicked it open, scrabbling with her still-locked seatbelt in her eagerness to get out and shout at whoever had caused the hold-up in the road.

"Don't cause an argu-" Jean began, but the door slammed in her face and Geri was already striding towards a couple who were looking at something in the road.

This wasn't the first time in their lives that Jean had sent a silent prayer to the sky that Geri wasn't about to get them both killed. She was feisty, with the shortest fuse of anyone Jean had ever known. While Jean wasn't exactly a push-over (they'd both inherited a bit of spice from Columbian ancestors), she was more measured in her approach. Especially when it came to confrontations.

Jean got out of the car, surprised that the air wasn't filled with the sound of her sister's voice laying into the other drivers who had blocked their path. But the road was silent. Eerily so. She breathed in a wet animal stench—a mixture of sodden fur, muck, and piss that stuck in her throat as though the air itself had a physical presence.

Geri had joined the two spectators next to a Jeep Cherokee with the hood crumpled and steaming. Dark blood smeared the damaged grill. "Please let it be an animal," Jean whispered to herself as she strode to stand beside her sister.

Relief came she stepped close enough to see black fur. A bear? But the arm that lay prone on the tarmac ended with a greyish-white palm, five fingers topped with blunt nails curled upwards, as though it had just palmed a baseball. The hand was human-like but huge. One thing Jean knew, this was no bear.

The man she guessed had been driving the Cherokee looked up at her with wide, frightened eyes. "It just ran out. I didn't have a chance to stop. I can't believe this."

A small, red Honda was the second parked car, facing the other direction. The driver, a stocky, middle-aged woman wearing dusty cowboy boots, shook her head. "My daddy always said he'd seen one out here, but I thought he was just telling tales. I can't believe it's real."

Ashen-faced, the man clutched the back of his neck in clear distress.

Jean looked at the creature spreadeagled in the road. A sensation of panic gripped her muscles as her brain struggled to accept what she was seeing.

The sasquatch was dead. If it hadn't been obvious from the glaze of its eyes that stared up at the sky, so dark Jean could see the reflections of the clouds passing high above them, it was clear from the brain matter that leaked in a pulpy cream mass under its skull. Its head was conical in shape, reminding her of that old alien movie with Dan Aykroyd. A flap of furry skin was displaced from its scalp, the visible skin beneath pale and blue-hued.

The side of its body had taken the brunt of the car's impact and ribs the width of pool noodles were visible through the shaggy, blood-soaked hair. One of its legs was twisted, and its prominent whiteish-blue foot lay huge and unsullied in the road. Jean stared at its toes. At the dermal ridges that swirled around its heel. This was no prankster in a suit.

An overwhelming rush of emotion flooded her chest and she couldn't quite place it. She felt like crying, and blinked quickly, turning her gaze from the body to the spectators so she could take a breather and gather herself. "What do we do now?"

The woman wiggled her phone. "I called the cops. They're sending someone out. I'm Sheila, by the way. That's Jack."

Jean introduced herself and Geri, then asked, "What did you say to the cops?"

"The truth, not that the girl in despatch believed it. Talked to me like I was loopy on meth or somethin'."

Jack, in shock, visibly began to tremble. "Do you think I'll go to jail?"

"I told you, buddy. The way that thing ran out at you, there was no way you could have stopped."

"You saw it happen?" Jean asked Sheila.

"I was coming the other way, but I saw it alright. Looked like it was chasing something or something was chasing it, the way it pelted outta there."

The man wiped his eyes with shaking hands. "But aren't they protected or something? Will I get fined?"

"It isn't like you shot it," Sheila told him, firmly. "It was an accident."

There was the sound of approaching tires and a pale blue Camry pulled up behind Jean's car. She recognised the passengers from the rest stop—a father in his twenties and his son, a boy of around six years old. The boy had amused the sisters in the queue to the counter, firing bad joke after bad joke at his dad. From the man's reactions each time, Jean could tell most of the jokes had come from him in the first place.

There had been one quip that made Jean chuckle and seemed to take the dad by surprise. The boy had pointed toward the drink chiller. "Dad! Did you know Dr. Pepper was a real doctor?"

The father had looked at the bottles of soda in quiet contemplation for a moment, as though he wasn't sure if the boy was making a joke at all. "Was he?"

"Yeah, he was a FIZZ-ician! Get it? Like a physician but fizzy? Because it's soda!"

Despite the over-telling that certainly took the momentum out of the joke, Jean couldn't help but smile.

The dad stared at his son for a moment with a look of bemused wonder on his face. It was an expression that asked where in the hell his kid had heard it. Then he broke into a shrill laugh, unmistakably real in comparison to the stream of fake laughter he'd forced at the other jokes.

Now, the boy leapt from the car and hit the ground running. His father tried to grab him but missed. The child's small feet were loud slaps in the stunned and eerie silence of those standing sentinel around the creature's body.

When the boy saw the sasquatch, he screamed.

The father finally caught up and hauled the kid up

against his chest. The initial scream over and forgotten, the boy wriggled in the man's arms, trying to look again at the mangled mystery on the highway.

"This is some kind of joke…a man in a suit," he mumbled over his son's hair.

"It's real, alright," Sheila said. "We've called the authorities."

"Who, Mulder and Scully?" the man retorted, unable to take his eyes off the body.

Geri tugged at Jean's sleeve. "I've gotta *go*," she whispered, urgently.

All thoughts of her sister's full bladder had vanished at the sight of the creature, but Jean now turned her attention back to the matter at hand. Geri looked queasy with the pressure, shifting her weight from foot to foot and holding her swollen waistband.

"So go behind a tree," Jean muttered.

"You have to come with me."

"Why?" Jean snapped. "You're twenty-four, not fourteen, Ger."

Her sister poked a finger at the beast. "What if there's more out there? What if this guy's family think I killed it? And you heard what she said, it looked like it was running away from something. What if there's another monster out there that's even bigger?"

"That was just a figure of speech. She didn't mean it."

Geri moaned, hunching over. "Please!"

With an exasperated hiss, Jean pushed her sister toward the woods and followed, marching her along with a firm hand against her shoulder. "Just go here," she said once they'd stepped into the tree line.

Geri looked over her shoulder, a frantic panic in her

eyes. "I can still see those people. If I can see them, they might see me."

"Nobody is interested in watching you piss in a bush, Ger!" But she dutifully followed her sister as she scurried into the longer brush, already fumbling with the zipper of her shorts.

When Geri was finally satisfied, she crouched and let out an agonised wail as she forced her brain to override the order to clench against the flow.

Jean winced in sympathy and turned her attention back to the group. They had stopped looking down at the creature and were shielding their eyes from the sun, heads tilted toward the road ahead. Jean heard the rumbling of an approaching engine. "I think the cops might be here," she said.

"Huh?" Geri grunted, squeezing out the last, agonising drips.

"It looks as though the cops are here."

"Do you have a tissue?"

"No."

"Well, what the hell am I going to wipe with?"

"Why is this my fault?"

Geri swore. "Gimme your sock?"

Jean shifted her position, trying to get a better view of the road. She didn't even bother to respond to that particular request. The creature was the most exciting thing she had ever seen, and she was stuck in the woods acting as a restroom attendant for her obnoxious sister. The roar of a deep engine cut out, and she heard multiple car doors slam shut.

"Can you at least get me a big leaf or something?" The snapping of twigs behind her made Geri forget all about wiping. She yanked her pants up, lurching towards Jean and away from the sounds. "What was that?"

Jean shushed her. The hairs on her arms were standing on end. It sounded as though something large was edging closer, just beyond the thicket. Her mind raced, imagining a huge, angry bigfoot lunging out of the bushes and tearing them to shreds for being a party to the harming of its friend. She began to walk backwards, pulling Geri with her. "Let's just back away and get to the cops," she gritted out, relieved that the cavalry was so close.

A gunshot rang out through the trees. Down the road, startled birds flooded the sky. Geri's knee crashed into Jean's thigh as they both crumpled down into the grass and then lay flat, facing the road.

Sheila screamed for a moment before the piercing shout was silenced by another shot.

"Did the monster wake up?" Geri asked, her body trembling against Jean's side.

"They aren't shooting the bigfoot," Jean said the words, but her brain didn't want to believe it. She'd seen Jack fall, the side of his skull split open by the first bullet. He'd landed on top of the creature.

Two more bullets sounded, and Jean forced herself to try and forget that the child and his father were there.

"Stay down," Jean told her sister, firmly. Hopefully hidden from sight in the long grass, she listened, on high alert.

An Australian voice barked disinterested orders. "Get this stupid hairy fuck in the back of the truck first. That's three in as many months. What the hell are they playing at?"

"It's the distortion pulse confusing them, boss." A woman's voice. Through the blades of grass, Jean watched a blonde in military gear tug out Jack's wallet while three burly men set to work wrapping the bigfoot in a white tarp.

"The pulses are supposed to keep them off the roads and send them straight into the drop traps, so we don't have shit like this to clean up every time."

"Yeah, well. They aren't working." The woman rifled through Sheila's pockets and looked over at the cars. "Boss? We've got three adults and four cars, here."

"Shit!" Jean hissed, forcing herself down lower. It was futile. If the soldiers came looking for them, they would have to try their luck running.

"Maybe some of them were riding together?" the man spoke.

After a pause, the blonde pointed out, "But, that would mean we have even more witnesses unaccounted for."

"Right, right...just testing," the man who was in charge peered out into the treeline and raised his gun. For a dreadful moment, Jean thought he had seen them. She braced herself for the searing punch of a bullet in the top of her skull, wrapping her arms tighter around her sister.

There was a crunch as a large boot stepped into the bracken.

"They're coming," Geri hissed.

More footsteps sounded, moving to the right of them this time. The soldiers—or whoever these people were—were flanking them, trying to drive them out. There was no way they could stay put.

"We have to run," Jean whispered into her sister's hair.

Geri shook her head, terror overwhelming rationality.

Over the long grass, the female soldier's face came into view, her head turned and scanning the tree line, but Jean knew it wouldn't be long before she clocked them lying there.

"Remember what Grandma said to do if someone starts shooting. Split up and run in a zigzag, get somewhere far enough away, then hide. We have to run into the trees. Go. Go now!" Jean hauled her sister to her feet and shoved her deeper into the woods.

They both broke into a crouched sprint, trying and failing to remain soundless.

"There!" someone shouted, and a shot blasted, punching a small hole in the tree just in front of Jean and sending scattered splinters of bark into her cheeks as she pelted past it.

Every second, she expected a bullet to tear into her skull, but the path she was cutting through the woods appeared to be working.

Geri was still barefoot and began to slow, limping in pain.

"Keep going!" Jean gasped.

Crying, her eyes wide in disbelief, Geri's lips drew back over her teeth as she hissed air into her lungs, the expression of a primate under attack. A hole exploded in her cheek, blood spraying the trees, the force of the shot sending her spinning to the ground.

Jean screamed and U-turned, falling on her knees beside the body.

Geri's body.

Her baby sister's body.

If only she'd let her pee in the car, Jean's inner monologue tortured her. She could have filled up that Big Gulp cup and thrown it out the window and they might not have stopped because Jean had her eye on the road and might have got one of those gut feelings she often had that saved them from danger. They could have swerved around Jack's Jeep and left the carnage in the dust. The alternative scenarios flooded her mind as she looked down at Geri, crumpled and bloodied on the woodland floor.

"Too bad about your friend," a voice spoke behind her. There was a click.

Before Jean even had time to brace herself, something screeched and launched itself at the man holding the gun out toward Jean's forehead. It was a black blur, a smudge of feral rage. A gorilla on the rampage but Jean knew that wasn't quite it. It was as terrifying and as primal as a silverback on the attack. But it was bigger. So much bigger.

Instincts kicked in, and Jean ran. Shots rang out behind her but this time she knew she was the least of the gunmen's worries. Something sailed through the air and landed, rolling, ahead of her.

The gunman's head.

She kicked it on the way past, a fractional moment of satisfaction blooming dopamine in her haywire nervous system. The fleeting rush was short-lived.

Jean hit a wall.

It wasn't a physical wall. She could still see the trees ahead of her and the breeze tousling her hair also shimmied the leaves in her pathway. But something caused her whole body to freeze. The world began to spin. She covered her ears, aware of a high-pitched, unnatural buzz coming from somewhere nearby.

The distortion pulse, she realised, remembering what the Australian had said.

She staggered, tears streaming, vomit erupting from her without warning. Knowing she had to get out of the range of the disorientating rays if she had any chance of making it through the woods, Jean tried to run.

Her body shambled along as though the floor was the deck of a ship caught in a tumult. She tipped from side to side and shoulder-barged trees, landing on her hands and knees. Each time she dragged herself up, skinning her hands on the bark, and ambled on.

The pounding bursts of electric distortion sent hammer blows through her skull and she threw up again, choking on stringy bile as she forced herself to continue her capering sprint toward safety.

A flash of light caught her eye, coming through the trees not a hundred feet ahead. It was sunlight on moving chrome. A road!

Jean sobbed with relief, spitting puke that flew back in her face as she staggered forward.

It was a busy highway, and she could see the cars now. Colours flew past the tree trunks and she heard the high and low rumblings of engines of varying sizes.

Fifty feet away and she knew she could make it. It felt like her heart might explode and her brains were scrambled, but she was almost out of the woods. Someone would pick her up before any surviving hunters caught her. She could disappear and hope that they assumed the rampaging bigfoot had killed her, too.

She was within eyesight of passengers now; she just

knew it. She fought to lift her arms and began to wave.

The earth under her feet turned to mush, and she fell through the woodland floor.

Under the pulse of the hideous distortion rays, she felt well, but just for those few fragile seconds between the tumble and the landing.

A searing burst of agony ripped through her thigh. Another sliced through her shoulder and into her cheek.

She had landed, but somehow, she was still suspended.

Rolling her eyes to try and see where she had fallen, Jean recoiled in horror.

She was in a pit of sharpened wooden pikes. One had plunged through the meat of her thigh, holding her aloft two feet above the pit floor. The other had dislocated her shoulder, pushed through her chest and come to rest in her cheek, the point pressing into her back upper molar. Every time she breathed, the wood caressed raw nerve and tissue, sending sickening shockwaves through her nervous system.

Her situation was dire, but the scene that met her in the pit was almost worse than being impaled herself. If she had somehow landed on her feet between two of the spikes, miraculously unharmed, she might still wish she had died in the fall.

The sasquatches lay dead and dying, five at first count, more if she took in the skulls and bones that scattered the ground beneath her prone body.

They were in various states of decay. Some had black fur that peeled away in places to reveal unfathomable muscle and almost comically huge bone. The stench was unspeakable and the sweet, rancid tang of death overpowered the scent of the forest pines above.

It was a tragedy beyond words. Directly opposite her lay a baby bigfoot with a spike piercing through its ribcage. It was the same height as the little boy who told the jokes from the convenience store. The sasquatch was alive, staring at her with wide, frightened eyes that held the innocence of a child. In that moment Jean felt more sympathy for the creature than for herself. They did not deserve this.

Although her thigh was caught on a spike, the back of her heel rested on something soft. A huge sasquatch lay curled near her feet, a dry puddle of blood under its head.

A shadow fell over the pit. Looking up, Jean could see a figure. The Australian peered down, rifle in hand.

This is it, Jean realised. She was about to be shot. *Death will be nothing at all, or I will be with Geri*, she told herself, firmly.

A metallic clang rang out and something began to move over the hole.

Terror was not enough. The feeling that overtook Jean was so much more.

The Australian waved as the drop-floor canopy was slowly replaced and the pit was plunged into darkness.

Somewhere in the stinking black, there was a whimper.

Jean reached out and touched her finger to the soft pad of the young bigfoot's hand. They cried together amongst the bones.

Later, Jean woke blearily to waves of pain, her heartbeat slowing as blood loss and shock shut down her organs. Her foot lifted, pushed by the something soft that it had been resting on. She couldn't muster the energy to scream at the pain of her leg being pushed back up the pike as the creature clambered to its feet. She could smell it looming over her. Its stomach rumbled in the darkness.

It sniffed at the blood that dripped down from her wounds.

Pain exploded over her shoulder as it chomped down. Jean's scream was loud and shrill, but nobody could hear it. Her cries were swallowed up by the sounds of the traffic passing by just metres away from the pit.

Stooge

Compared to the downtown hovel of the gentleman's club Evan performed in each night, the funeral parlour smelled like a dream. Although the formaldehyde stench of chemicals mixed with drain water was wafting under a nearby door (made even more noticeable by the lack of mourners attending), the church-like cosiness of dusty pews and the springtime pollen of the few drooping bunches of flowers near the coffin gave the room a sense of occasion.

The occasion was Evan's mother's funeral.

He'd hopped straight on a plane from his last show, still wearing his magician's suit as it was the only thing he owned that was remotely appropriate. The suit was a dark, pinstriped grey, sized slightly too large to conceal his tricks in hidden pouches within the lining, and the right flap gaped open on his thigh, revealing creamy satin. A dark bloodstain had dried to a crusted brown. Evan winced and straightened the jacket, covering the mark. He glanced around the room, hoping nobody had seen the dubious-looking stain. But there was barely anybody in the room at all, let alone anyone close enough to spy a bloodstain on a hapless magician's inner jacket lining.

It wasn't what it looked like. That is, it was blood, but it wasn't human.

Evan's magic show was built on the macabre, as was his family's tradition. His cup-and-balls routine began with sheep eyes and grew to a grotesque finale where he slapped a blood-soaked bull's heart on the table. In his opinion, it beat the hell out of Paul Daniels' orange. But the punters at Fat Frank's Fiddles and Fries were usually too wasted to offer any appreciation. Of the latest heckles, a demand to, "Eat it! Eat the fucking heart, you pointless fuck!" haunted him each night as he prepared to step on the sticky, threadbare carpet of the stage.

While the sheep eyes he used in his routine were glass replicas that had been passed down in his grandfather's trick box, and the animal skulls that increased in size as the trick progressed didn't leave any residue, he honoured his father's wish to continue the tradition of a truly show-stopping finale. Because of this, he ordered a real bull's heart from the butchers two days before every show. He'd spent more on that damn trick than he'd earned in his life, but to him it was worth it. The rare occasions when someone in the audience gasped or gagged at the horrific reveal of a shining and bloodied bull's heart was worth losing everything for.

At thoughts of the latest heart, he cringed a little. He'd received the news of his mother's death just after returning to his shitty apartment and had thrown a few meagre belongings into a bag, leaving his trick case in the living area. How long until the stench of rotten flesh brought concerned neighbours to call the cops and break down the door? In his part of the city, probably not before he returned. He didn't relish the idea of airing out a room that had housed the rotting heart in the heat of the Vegas summer. Nor did he have the funds to pay for a new door if his apartment was raided. Of the lesser of two evils, he'd face the rancid, maggot-infested heart any day.

At his side, a concealed pocket housed a long scarf he had printed to look like crime scene tape for his cut and restore act. In his fantasies, he pulled up an audience member to lie on the ground like a corpse while he performed the trick over them, acting like a detective waiting for the forensic crew to show before the murderer returned. It was a cool act, fast and witty. His skill at the restoration illusion had improved in the last couple of years, and he would have loved to showcase it the way he'd imagined countless times. But the three times he'd asked for audience participation had been disastrous. The first had headbutted him out of the blue and for no apparent reason. When Evan had staggered up to Fat Frank to see what could be done about the assault, blood streaming down his chin, the club owner had snorted, sending droplets and crusts of snot into the bristles of his moustache.

"You're a Z-list magician in Vegas, kid. What the hell did you expect?"

The second time, the eager and willing audience member had gone out of their way to show Evan up, matching his tricks and showboating to the audience.

That one hurt even more than the headbutt. One thing he'd learned that night: magicians were a dime a dozen in his city. And he wasn't as talented as he thought he was.

After the third incident, he'd vowed never to use an audience member in a trick until he'd made it big.

That was seven years ago.

He was still at Fat Frank's Fiddles and Fries and, although the club's exterior was Irish-themed, the 'fiddles' part of the name didn't refer to an instrument. The punters who packed the dark and smoke-filled room at night were enticed by the sign on the door that advertised jobs for 18+ girls who could dance. *Get paid more if you look less!* read the sign's sickening draw. At first, he'd wondered why Frank bothered hiring a magician's act at all. That was until the night he pulled a young man on stage who had readily followed his instructions until, halfway through the cut-and-restore, the guy had pointed an angry finger at Evan and accused him of being a front for a trafficking ring.

Evan had gawped. Is that really what was going on? Could he be so naïve he couldn't see that Frank hired him so that it seemed like a legitimate club, distracting prying eyes from the depravity happening in the back rooms?

Sometimes, late at night, Evan thought about that young man who had been desperately trying to find out what happened to his missing sister, Gabby. When the kid had thrust the photograph of a young girl who had started as a waitress and soon progressed to hostess before vanishing one night, Evan pretended he hadn't ever met her. He'd dated one of the dancers over the years, a quiet and brooding girl who he convinced himself he didn't love but whose apartment he found himself at with the repetitive urgency of a smack addict to their dealer. April (born in May but already named for her perceived due date) had known Gabby well and had a pretty good idea about where she had gone. Every few weeks a car crept into the parking lot behind Fat Frank's and a girl was invited to audition for a shot at a better life. The touts were besuited, usually women with kind faces, and the girls were awed at the chance to get away from the dead-end grind that being on the lowest rung of Vegas's ladder brought.

"Where do you think they go?" Evan had asked, stroking April's leg on one oppressively hot afternoon. April's bedroom was on the second floor, and the sun burned an apocalyptic haze through the gauze of her flimsy curtains. As a result, their lovemaking was lazy and slow, with countless hours spent recovering in tangled blankets, sweat glinting as it dried on their bare skin.

"Nowhere good," April had replied, determined never to fall into the trap set by the wolves that prowled for girls who clung to hope even as they strolled the back alleys of Vegas's seediest clubs.

Six months after that conversation, April had Evan's baby. She moved closer to her parents, taking the boy with her. To his shame, Evan had been relieved. He was too busy to be a father and magic had always been his true love. Last he'd heard, April was a manager at a rotating bar in Seattle and the boy, Rex, was good at maths and Mandarin. When he'd read these factoids after glancing at the photograph of a smiling three-year-old with missing teeth and a dimple in his chin that mirrored his own, he'd felt even further removed from his role as a parent. He wanted to be a magician above all else, just like all the men in his family. He would do anything to fulfil his legacy.

Even if it meant cutting ties with his entire living family.

Looking up at the coffin resting on a stark black frame at the front of the room, Evan felt a pang of regret. Although the woman had been called Margory, the flower wreath simply read 'Marge', a nickname she had never called herself. The expense of the wreath was by letter, and he couldn't afford the R and Y. He may be cheap, but nothing could match the disappointment Margory had shown at hearing he was pursuing a career in illusionism. Evan could still feel the sting of his mother's slap across his cheek.

He'd recoiled in shock, tears blurring his last image of the woman who'd brought him up on her own since his father vanished when he was four years old.

"How can you do this to me?" she'd whispered. "How can you do this to yourself?"

"There is no such thing as a curse, Mom!" he'd called over his shoulder as he stormed to his room and packed his belongings.

"You've doomed us both!" she'd yelled, and he had snorted at her dramatics. That turned out to be the last thing she ever said to him. A couple of years after their falling out, he had tried to call, attempting to mend the bridge. But she had stayed silent, her angered breathing hissing down the phone. She hung up first, without saying a word. He pictured her, standing under the hideous painting of Christ on the Cross that had been passed down through her family. She had grown more and more religious after his father went missing, her fear of the curse spurring her to counteract it with prayer.

When Evan's mother had married his father, she hadn't believed in curses, either. The Great Aldo, the grandson of the legendary Cornelius Robeux and child of Desmond the Deceptive (who had died in an unfortunate incident on stage at age 32), had been a former hit on the stage of a historic venue in the back alleys of Vienna. His glistening career had inexplicably nosedived and ended with him working sleight-of-hand to keep the pensioners from revolting when their food was delayed on a cruise ship. One rainy night, sitting under the canopy of their balcony somewhere in the Adriatic, he'd told her about his family history and the curse that plagued him.

At first, Margory—whose body now lay in the wooden box at the front of the room, slightly bloated and smoother than it had been thanks to the formaldehyde and setting agents—had laughed. Margory did not believe in curses. Margory believed that any family who decided to use magic as their main form of income were the very definition of *making your own luck*. But she'd loved Aldo and so humoured his long-held belief that the men in his family were destined to be both magicians and doomed to die young and in terror.

The reason for this supposed curse originated not too far in the annals of Evan's family history when his great-grandfather had done a terrible, terrible thing. Evan had read his father's account of the incident when he'd found his diaries in a box in the garage. His dad's journals had read like the fever dream of a crazed drunk in the grasp of hallucinations.

Cornelius Robeux was the most pretentious fake name of any magician Evan had met, closely followed by Desmond the Deceptor (real name Daryl). However, Cornelius was the true birth name of the man whose actions purportedly cursed every male in his bloodline. He was a practised and skilled magician and, like many of that time, he had learned his skills during a stint in prison for an undisclosed misdemeanour. Whatever the crime, the seven years inside had given Cornelius countless hours to perfect moves including his back palm, steal, and pull. He'd moved on from basic card tricks in his first year of incarceration and, by the time he walked out a free man, his conjuring skills were legendary. So much so that he had his own show, spectator payments being made in cigarettes and food from his fellow inmates. This enabled him to save his cash rather than spend it in the commissary. With his savings, he set up a small stage show in the East End of London that snowballed in popularity. Cornelius was mysterious, aggressive, and cold. The Victorian audience was used to being pandered to, and the apparent disinterest of the man on the stage caused the men to attempt to fault him at every turn and the women to question whether they would prefer their husbands to be a little less gentlemanly behind closed doors.

Cornelius used an audience stooge for his finest trick. His stooge was one of two men that Cornelius had ever trusted, making him a perfect ally for his stage act. The men had met in the prison and become firm friends. The stooge received a cut of the audience fees and a promise that Cornelius would never shiv him in an argument, a promise that Cornelius made to few.

Their trust was irrevocably broken one windy autumn night, the gentle creaking of the wood in the rafters above adding atmosphere to Cornelius's favourite trick; a levitation. He had called his stooge out of the audience to watch from the side of the stage and act as though there was no trickery afoot. It had been going as well as always until an audience member suddenly cried, "Fraud!" The outburst was met with a flurry of titters.

Cornelius had faltered. "Not so, I assure you. For how would you explain this?"

As he acted out the side-to-side move that had formerly set the crowd into astonished squeals, someone in the balcony called down. "Isn't it just a carnival trick? A concealed board that you manoeuvre behind a mirror that reflects the stage?"

The magician had lowered himself, the crowd in uproar. "But I have here a witness who can confirm that there is no trickery afoot."

He turned to the stooge, but his most trusted companion's expression told him all he needed to know. The man's face was sweaty and pink, his eyes darting to the people who had called out from the audience whom he clearly recognised. The guilt was evident.

While Cornelius had noted the stale beer on his assistant's breath that day, he had thought nothing of it provided he could still perform as required. Putting two-and-two together under the jeering laughter of the audience, Cornelius understood what had occurred. During a moment of drunken, attention-seeking bravado, his stooge had told the people in the public house the secret behind Cornelius's levitation act.

And so, there was nothing for it but grave revenge.

Cornelius played the long game. He acted as though he had seen a rival conjurer in the audience the previous night, and surmised to the stooge that it must have been he who was trying to sully his name.

They began to work on a new trick and, to satisfy the stooge's ever-growing thirst, Cornelius kept the rehearsal room stocked with liquor.

He chose a trick that would require little acting by his stooge. During his studies of the books in the prison library, Cornelius had read of a phenomenon called the body transfer illusion. A way of bamboozling the brain into believing it is seeing and feeling a limb that doesn't belong to it.

The trick begins simply enough. The magician has an audience member or, in Cornelius's case, his stooge, sit in a chair with his arms resting on a table in front of him. He takes one of the participant's arms and hides his shoulder under a blanket. A wooden frame is used to conceal the arm from the man's sight, although the audience can still observe it. The hidden arm is replaced with a replica that the participant can see (Cornelius had a human arm cast in porcelain for his act). From here, the magician uses two feathers and carefully works his way over each finger of the stooge's hand both behind the screen and on the fake hand. He's careful to ensure that each touch of the feather lands in the same part of the hands at the exact same time. The hidden ring finger and the visible porcelain ring finger must get a sweep of the feather tip as one. The real index knuckle must tickle at the same time he tickles the index knuckle of the dummy hand. Soon, the brain becomes confused. It believes the fake hand is the real hand, as it cannot see the antics of the magician behind the screen.

Cornelius told the stooge that he would end the act as it had been done on countless occasions. He would slam a mallet down on the porcelain hand, shattering it. They did not rehearse this part, as he wanted the stooge's sheer shock, manipulated pain impulse, and reaction to be completely raw and unversed.

Their first performance back after the crowd shouted Cornelius's secrets, he closed the show with his new illusion.

It went according to plan.

Completely unaware that he was under suspicion, the stooge was happy to sit in the audience and wait for his turn to be called up. He'd gratefully accepted the outfit Cornelius had supplied him with earlier in the day, his mentor promising that the suit's design would emphasise the fake hand. He apologised that he had spilt some vodka on the material earlier and that the alcohol smell would soon fade. The stooge, already five vodkas deep himself, did not notice the strange mist of sharp ethanol lingering around him.

When called upon, the stooge had clambered onto the stage with an awed and grateful expression. He looked a little confused that the chair and the floor around it were covered in rock salt that crunched under his shoes, but when Cornelius began the act, the stooge visibly relaxed, waiting for his cues.

As was his style, Cornelius twisted the narrative to encourage the audience to believe that the porcelain hand was haunted and that the spirit was now attached to the stooge's soul. He explained that the salt had been placed around the man for protection against the vagrant spirits, as one might salt a doorway. The stooge laughed when the feather tickled his pottery hand, completely genuine in feeling. He flinched when Cornelius whipped out the mallet at the end and proceeded to tap each knuckle, the way a physician tests reflexes.

The finale, or so the stooge believed, was the moment Cornelius slammed the hammer down on the fake hand, smashing it to pieces with a satisfying explosion of hollow pottery.

The attack caused the stooge to yelp and push his chair back, his real hand leaping from under the blanket, flailing and knocking over the partition. He held his unharmed hand to his chest in bewildered awe, staring at his palm as the audience fell about laughing at his expense.

"I hear the call of the owner of the cursed arm," Cornelius told the crowd, holding fingers to his brow as though the voice was calling from within his skull. The audience hushed and the stooge, still cradling his uninjured hand, looked to his boss in puzzlement. They had not rehearsed this part. However, since they hadn't rehearsed the hammer blow either, he trusted Cornelius, as any fool would.

The stooge shuffled his chair back to the table and, when prompted, returned his arms to the surface. He looked excited, as eager as the audience to see what Robeux had planned.

"I fear I may have made a grave mistake," Cornelius

said in an ominous tone. "The dark spirits that resided in the arm were released upon its destruction. They have consorted and now cling to our friend, here."

Unusually for Cornelius, he hammed to the audience at this point with a jovial wink. They laughed and applauded, on his side now the man in the chair was being made a fool of.

The stooge looked nervous, fighting the urge to whisper queries about the unusual turn the act had taken.

Cornelius continued. "I'm hearing more from the spirits of the arm. I regret we may be dealing with something extremely dark."

In the audience, women gasped. Men coughed, trying to hide their fearful discomfort with the only exclamation accepted by their peers.

"In many cultures since the dawn of human existence, fire has been used to eradicate and to cleanse. While we all know the dangers of the fires of hell, perhaps we can pre-empt such a sorrowful end by destroying the sins that the hand has passed on to this poor soul. I believe the only way to appease the spirits will be by cleansing." At this, Cornelius whipped out a single, long match.

There are a few remaining accounts of this astonishing trick, told on postcards for visiting tourists and in diaries from witnesses who mused long after about how it was done.

The only thing known for sure is that Cornelius struck the match and waved it over the man's arm. It didn't touch the material, nor did it set his clothes alight.

But soon, the stooge began to writhe. He patted his hand over the 'burning' arm, then reacted as though the invisible fire had passed to his other sleeve.

Cornelius stood back, presenting the spectacle as the stooge screamed and leapt from the chair. Every time he attempted to put out the fire with his hands, it appeared to spread further. He bent down and rubbed at his trousers, squealing.

Over his screams, Cornelius addressed the audience. "All folly, of course, but the man is still under my power! As you can see, there is no fire."

The stooge was screaming now, and the audience was laughing.

"For my final trick, I will show you a vision of the devilish creature contained within the arm!"

Cornelius waved his hands and wafted them over the stooge, who was now on his knees on the stage, wailing and choking. The salt on the ground appeared to cause his knees agony, only heightening the illusion of demonic activity.

The hair on his head began to singe. The skin on his face turned red and bubbled.

The audience screamed with him, somewhere in the middle of delight and disgust.

"Please!" the stooge cried. "I'm on fire!"

The audience cackled with delight, pointing and laughing with awe at the spectacle. There was still no fire to be seen, although the pinking of all visible flesh continued, the stooge's hands clawed and boiling.

"Then I shall be sure to put you out!" Cornelius said. He tossed two large buckets of salt over the man and smothered him in a thick woollen blanket. The audience tittered, thrilled.

"Now, I banish you!" Cornelius yelled. He pressed a

hand to the stooge's forehead and kicked the hidden lever that sent the man dropping backwards under the stage in a hiss of smoke. The audience erupted and Cornelius's legacy was reborn.

Cornelius checked on the stooge just once directly after the show, making sure the invisible fire caused by the suit soaked in ethanol was truly out, and that the punishment wasn't going to burn the theatre down. Cornelius still had to make a living, after all. The stooge was cowering in a corner under the stage in the darkness, illuminated only by the strips of light coming through the gaps in the floorboards. His skin was pink, with a mottling of singed black. The rest of his flesh wept with agonised-looking blisters that oozed yellow fluid and sat above flesh that barely clung to the bone beneath.

Following the show's success, Cornelius had been invited to travel to a theatre in Paris. He informed the agent that he would never re-enact the devilry part of the final trick, because it had greatly disturbed the poor man he'd picked at random from the audience.

Knowing that he no longer needed the theatre and with a body to dispose of, he burnt the theatre to the ground, anyway.

His vengeance complete, Cornelius thought little of the stooge. However, one observation when he'd peered into the crawl space and seen the dying man had troubled him. Chalk had been a common component for tricks in those days, and the stooge must have found a stub under the stage. During the hours he lived, his skin still burning although the invisible fire had long died out, he mustered his final ounce of strength to write on the wood.

And what he wrote, Cornelius didn't understand.

He hadn't known much about his stooge, other than his alcohol dependence, and gullibility. But the one thing he should have bothered to ask was the reason why he had been incarcerated. Cornelius had assumed that the other criminals on his floor had been captured for taking part in petty crimes, as he had. But there had been something decidedly more sinister about the stooge's practices.

Unknown to Cornelius, the stooge had been incarcerated all those years prior due to an odd series of events. A complaint that the man had been responsible for the death of a cat had filtered through his village, speculation growing when an animal's heart was found nailed to the church door that weekend. A groundskeeper at the church complained that a fresh body had been disturbed and, when the grave was excavated to see what might have been done to the corpse, they found it missing a hand.

Due to the suspicions about the cat, the police went directly to the stooge's house and discovered a shrine of sorts, the hand carved with strange symbols and pentagrams. He was incarcerated for theft from the graveyard, a crime that was decidedly difficult to punish as there was little precedence known in the village for such activities. However, in the annals of the court records there is a transcript that reads, *"Cyril Armstrong, 27, 4 months hard labour. Desecration of corpse. Satanic practices."*

Evan left the service in a daze, wavering from the curving path and stepping into the long grass, immediately soaking his pant leg with the burst of summer rain that had fallen during the interment.

He swore and patted his jacket, searching for cigarettes. He pulled out a pack of cards he'd marked and repackaged and swore under his breath.

A slender hand extended a packet of Marlboro in front of his eyes, and, when he took a smoke, the man made a lighter appear with the sleight of hand of a trained illusionist. Evan gratefully lit the cigarette and handed back the lighter. He walked beside the man as they exited the grounds.

The man was roughly Evan's height but a little slimmer. He had brown hair that curled slightly at the nape of his neck. It was impossible to tell his age. At a glance, the flesh of his face held deep grooves that could have come from years of smiles and frowns. But his eyes were bright and youthful, pale green in colour, with pupils ringed with jagged hazel spikes that made Evan think of his mother's hideous painting of Christ on the Cross.

He wore a long peacoat that swayed with the turning of his slender hips as he walked. With such grace, it came as no surprise to Evan when the man told him he was also a magician. "I was a huge fan of your grandfather's."

"You seem too young to have even heard of him."

"We've all grown up knowing the names Houdini, Kellar, and Thurston. Cornelius Robeux was no different for me."

Evan accepted the answer easily. Just as football fans could name entire teams from decades before their birth, fans of magic pored over the original illusionists and reports of their performances like collectors. There was no new trick, not really. Simply a new spin on the old techniques. Learning all you could about the first known magic tricks and the ones that followed could stand any creative magician on a course to success. However minimal and non-lucrative that success might be.

"It's an honour for me to be in your presence, truly. I've read about the history of your relatives and watched your career with great interest." The man lowered his head. "I was saddened to hear of the passing of your mother. I conversed with her a few times, and she offered a great deal of advice to me when I was compiling my show."

Evan frowned. That did not sound like Margory, although perhaps her vitriol at magicians was reserved only for those who shared part of her DNA profile.

The man caught his expression and let out a soft laugh. "Of course, her advice mostly consisted of encouragement to run toward any profession other than magic. But in the moments when I was able to show her some of my work, she enjoyed recalling the times she had worked with your father on his act. I believe there was something akin to nostalgia in her eyes when she corrected my positioning or advised how to conceal a clumsy force."

Envy, red and raw, bloomed in Evan for a moment. How wonderful it would have been to be able to perform for his mother and have her pass on directly the skills she grew to know from living with his father.

"Would you like to see what we worked on the last time I saw her?" the man asked.

"I don't even know your name," Evan said. He was struggling with post-funeral haze. It was as though the world had momentarily turned to treacle, and he was wading through it with his entire body, somehow able to breathe into black-coated lungs.

Extending a slim hand, the man beamed and declared with the theatricality that could only indicate a stage name. "I am Pelinore Phasmagore! Or Gore, to my friends."

"And may I call you Gore?"

"Any relative of the great Cornelius Robeux is an instant friend of mine. You may."

"Then, Gore, I would be honoured to see your trick." He shook the peculiar man's hand. The magician was trying a little too hard to fit the persona of a Victorian illusionist, Evan thought, biting back irritation. The plummy patter of his speech was far too much for the modern world but since he idolised Cornelius it was little surprise he'd adopted this style.

"How marvellous. I am staying at a lodging on the other side of the river. Would you like to come this way?"

Evan walked with the man, listening as he spoke in great detail about his grandfather's tricks with a level of detail that even Evan himself hadn't known.

"Here we are!" Gore whipped a key from his pocket and opened a green door, pushing it through a pile of discarded mail. "Never mind about all that."

Evan stepped over the footprint-marked letters and

spied a name, Cyril Armstrong. He would perhaps have plumped for Pelinore himself if he'd been a budding magician named Cyril.

He was led into a small room with a chaise lounge. The bed was the colour of a snooker table, the fabric crushed velvet.

"Do sit!"

"This is where I watch the trick?" Evan asked, setting his backside on the firm cushions of the chair.

"Good sir, the trick has already begun. In fact, my trick began over a century ago, when I cursed your family to a life of certain failure and an afterlife of displacement."

Evan was slow to react, the treacle-thick air that had surrounded him since the funeral growing stronger. He blinked at his strange companion, confusion tightening his brow.

The magician was leaning close, staring into his eyes. The spiked ring still surrounded his pupils, only now it glowed pale red in the hazy daylight. A slender finger touched Evan's forehead as a whispered chant was uttered by the trickster. The stooge. Gleefully repeating the words that Cornelius had yelled on stage before plunging him through the trapdoor, Cyril pressed against Evan's forehead and yelled, "Now, I banish you!"

Evan fell backwards onto the chaise and dreamed that he was climbing on stage with Pelinore Phasmagore, the audience politely clapping as he stepped into a vanishing cabinet, spotlit in the centre of the stage.

Pelinore closed the door, his grin the last thing Evan saw before being plunged into black.

It was a box. That was all he knew at first.

The magicians' motifs were all around. Folded fabric, draping over the sides of the container that he had been placed inside. A floor that felt fragile to the press of a heel, as though there was a mirror underneath blankets concealing a secret escape.

Evan chuckled. He'd been the stooge for a couple of friends over the years. Had bided his time in hidden compartments and contorted himself to fit under-floor hubs more times than he'd like to remember. But this time he was truly discombobulated.

He felt as though he was floating in the darkness. The more time that went on, the more uncomfortable he felt.

There was a sound, and he could have sworn it was his own name. It wafted through the empty black space like the thrumming of a distant train, true origins unclear.

"Hello?" he said into the dark, but either his ears were plugged, or his throat wouldn't work, and he couldn't make his voice anymore.

"Evan!"

The shout came from two different directions.

He turned around, the pull of vertigo rocking him on his feet. His face stared back through the black, his image cast on the shrouded mirror. The space behind him shimmered like reflections of a dark pool in glass. Lifting a heavy palm, he pushed it out in front of him. There was a wall of a mercury-like substance, and it swallowed the skin of his fingers. When he pulled back his hand the flesh was dry and the wall was intact. His reflection moved to the side without him budging an inch and he realised with a dropping sensation that it wasn't his reflection at all. Someone else was on the other side of the liquid wall. Someone who looked an awful lot like him.

"Dad?" Again, Evan's voice failed to make a sound, or his ears failed to hear it and he was still uncertain which it was because he could hear someone calling his name over and over.

The reflection that was not his reflection's face twisted in a miserable, soundless cry. Aldo punched his side of the wall with a balled fist, then slid to the ground in apparent anguish.

In the room to his father's left, Desmond the Deceptor watched his boy, the wall shimmering black. Evan stared at his grandfather, certain that he was in the grip of the most dreadful dream of his life.

"Evan!" a scream this time, from somewhere far across the black space. It was a woman's voice.

Dazed, Evan stepped away from the fluid wall and wandered over to where he thought the second voice had come from. There was another barrier, one which took him by surprise. He stepped right into the strange substance and it smothered him for a moment, seeping into his nose and clasping the sides of his neck before he jumped back in shock. Again, there were no droplets on his skin, and the substance retracted from his nostrils without leaving any residue.

A figure stepped up to the wall and placed flat hands on the surface.

The face emerged through the blackness.

It was his mother, and she was frantic. She spoke and

her words were an agonised rush through his eardrums, reverberating the fine hairs of his inner ear and rattling through his skull. The train was no longer distant, it was beside him on the track. "What did you do?" she screamed. "I warned you. You damned us both."

"Mother, I'm sorry!" Evan yelled.

Another voice came from behind him, and through the shimmer of another partition, Evan saw a man with a beard and bald pate, a pocket watch glinting against a dark waistcoat.

"Cornelius?"

The older magician cowered. "He's here!" he said with a wail, and Evan's relatives shrank away, hiding in the darkness of each of their interminable cells.

Additional shadows fell over the endless gloom of the block of rooms and cruel laughter shimmied the fluid walls. Giant in comparison to Evan and his family, the strange man with the crown-of-thorn eyes peered in at his cosmic pets. A huge hand clasped the colloidal walls and shook the cells, a cruel child taunting a pot full of ants. Evan was flung from wall to wall. He landed closer to the giant figure and stared up at him in horror.

As he watched, the man waved his fingers and uttered a spell, and another room formed beside Evan's. It was empty for a brief moment, but a figure soon appeared, crouched and disorientated.

The man stood and Evan took in his face. It was a mixture of his own, his mothers', and April's. He knew then that it was Rex. Surely it couldn't be, Evan thought in horror. Their child was only three. His boy, who was good at maths and Mandarin, but had still grown up to become a magician. Doomed to live out the family curse.

Evan's son, now an adult in his mid-forties, turned and rushed to the far wall. From his own nightmarish chamber of black, Evan couldn't see the figure on the far side of his son's cell, but Rex certainly could.

He approached the shimmering wall and another figure materialised moments later.

"Son?" Rex said.

We've Already Gone Too Far

The bar was perfectly situated for days when the weather turned and the kids dashed for shelter on the brief walk from town to their student accommodation. It was graduation week, and throngs of giddy twenty-somethings in their finest clothes, their hair flattened from mortarboard hats and heavy downpours, stumbled through the double doors of Reggie's Bar and Grill. The grill had long since been closed, and a wooden sign with rotting edges and faded green paint had been screwed into the wall under the establishment's sign, reading "No food here."

Local kids called it RBG's and enjoyed its slightly isolated location. There was little chance of running into a parent or teacher here. The regulars were battle-hardened and kept to themselves, slumped over pints of beer with empty shot glasses that multiplied as the hours ticked on. Lionel Spooler glanced up from his frothed glass when two kids stumbled through the doors late Thursday evening.

He recognised the girl. Brodie Sage rubbed her arms exaggeratedly, swiping rain spatters from her skin. It wasn't cold, but the torrential rainclouds had brought with them the ominous illusion of arctic winds and blizzard snows. Inside the bar, damp clothing rapidly drying had steamed the windows, causing passing headlights and brake lights to blur into neon-like patterns behind the fogged glass.

Accompanying Brodie was a classmate. A male, but their bumping of shoulders and comedically exaggerated expressions as they goofed over to the bar made Lionel believe that they would never be any more than friends. Good ones at that, Lionel appraised. Life-long, even, depending on how events would play out that night.

"What are you drinking, Danny?" Brodie asked the young man, slipping onto the seat two down from Lionel. She kicked off her heels and wrapped her toes around the stool's wooden footrest.

"Beer," the boy told the bartender, Stig, a man in his mid-forties with thinning hair scraped back into a slim ponytail that hung down between his shoulder blades in wispy curls.

It seemed to Lionel that the boy's head of hair was taunting Stig, Danny's thick brown curls standing up in unruly serpent waves, so dense that the raindrops sat on the mane like jewels. Once seated, Danny shook his wet hair like a labrador, scattering droplets onto the bar. Stig slid a beer with a weak head through the spatters, sloshing lager that carried cloud-like wisps of froth and bled into the rain, consuming it.

Stig fixed Brodie with an eagle stare. "You graduated

today?"

"Sure did," Brodie beamed, tugging her phone from her skirt pocket and proudly displaying a shot of her holding her rolled diploma, her mortarboard tassel stark gold against her long, black hair.

"You got any ID with you apart from that?"

Danny plucked out a wallet and offered his driver's licence.

"That's for you. What about her?"

The two kids glanced at each other, then Danny fixed Stig with puppy-dog eyes to go with his retriever mannerisms. "Come on, man. We just graduated in the same class. She forgot her ID. Cut her some slack?"

Stig swiped a weary hand over his mouth and let his shoulders fall. "You kids are killin' me. Bring your ID next time, okay?"

Without asking what she wanted, Stig poured Brodie a beer with a slightly better head than Danny's and begrudgingly took her cash.

When Stig had moved out of earshot, wandering over to serve a group on the other side of the bar, Brodie let out a relieved laugh. "Fuck, I didn't think we were going to get away with that."

"We didn't lie," Danny pointed out, licking his upper lip although there was no risk at all of getting a beer foam moustache with the dreadful pour Stig had executed. "He doesn't have to know you're a child prodigy."

"I prefer genius over prodigy, but I'll take it," Brodie held up her own beer and Danny tapped the side of his glass against hers in a half-assed cheers. The girl drank three long slugs and set the beer down. "I can't wait to get on that plane to Unilab. Get me to California and far away from this God-bothering, backwards, ass-hat of a town."

Lionel flicked his eyes toward the girl and she noticed. Her cheeks flushed and her expression darted into one of instant regret at the thought that she might have offended him. That was the thing about atheists, Lionel knew, they were often so much more considerate of others than the believers. When there's a big guy in the sky ready to forgive everything you say and do, being an asshole seemed to be an easy choice for many of the churchgoing masses.

"I didn't mean to offend you, Sir," Brodie said, her contrition completely genuine.

"Now why would you think I'm offended?"

Brodie placed her bare feet on the sticky floor of the bar and turned her stool towards him. It was another tick in Lionel's book. She was brilliant but didn't think she was any better than a low-life scruff sitting alone in a bar. At that moment, he wished he could protect her forever.

She looked at Lionel the way she looked at Danny. No pity. No judgement. He imagined Brodie Sage addressed everyone with the same respect. "I don't know for sure. But I'm sorry if I spoke out of turn."

"About the town or about God?"

The kid tilted her head and Lionel felt like he'd snared a pike on a long line. A rarity that would come with a battle but would be more than worth it in the end.

Danny was getting bored with watching the back of his friend's head. Less comfortable making conversation with strangers at the bar, he craned around Brodie, grinning a false smile. He thrust his hand out to Lionel. "I'm Danny."

"Okay." Humouring him, Lionel briefly grabbed his fingers and squeezed enough for it to hurt. To his credit, Danny maintained eye contact and didn't flinch.

Brodie waved Danny away, indicating she wasn't done finding out if she'd hurt someone's feelings. "About God," she said to Lionel.

Lionel shrugged. "It's a difficult subject. One that impacts everyone, even if you don't believe."

"I don't," Brodie told him. "I'm sorry, but I've lived my life in science. I don't see a place for spiritualism."

"What do you believe happens when you die?"

Danny set his palm flat on the bar, his fingers recoiling slightly in the beery swill and leaving three tracks on the surface. "This is getting a little dark. We're celebrating tonight."

Lionel fixed his eyes on Brodie. "You want to answer my question. Why would you ever let a friend stop you from answering such an important question?"

"I won't." Brodie punched Danny in the upper arm, hard enough for his eyes to water. "Can't you just let me talk to him for two more minutes?"

Lionel knew that he had her, then. When it came to religion, people who didn't believe were as passionate as people who did. But they always felt the need to justify their choice. It fascinated him. He liked Brodie, already. Her answer surprised him, however.

"I believe that people see ghosts," she said. "I believe that people have experiences where it seems like their loved ones are there and they can't explain it. I believe in déjà vu. And I believe that it's because of something scientific. Something greater than what we know. You don't have to believe in God to believe that people do see ghosts and have paranormal experiences. There could be a multitude of scientific reasons behind them. Stone tape theory, for example."

Agreeing with Brodie's analysis, Lionel summarised the theory. "Energy cannot die. Therefore, when a human dies their energy may transfer to objects that also have high vibrational energy, such as stone. Occasionally these objects may release their energy, and people with highly intuitive vision may see the release in the form of the person or animal. Science, but beautifully spiritual."

"Exactly." Brodie swallowed a deep slug of beer.

"You didn't answer my question though. What do you think happens when you die?"

Danny pivoted on his chair, the repeated question a step too far. He pulled Brodie back toward him and Lionel could hear him 'whispering' over the jukebox music. "He seems like a creep, let's move over there."

To Lionel's relief, Brodie shut her friend down. "This is the most interesting conversation I've had in months."

It was about to get all the more interesting, Lionel knew. He readied himself to tell his story.

When Brodie convinced Danny to let her finish the conversation, she turned back to Lionel in apology.

"So?" he asked for the third time. "What do you think happens when you die?"

"I think it's nothing," she said. "I think it's like the deepest sleep, the point where you can't dream, but forever."

"And what about you, Hot Shot?" Lionel asked Danny. He knew he needed to get them both on board if he was going to be able to tell his story.

Danny seemed surprised his opinion was warranted at all. "Urm...I *want* to believe."

"What the fuck does that mean?" This was Brodie, and the vitriolic response shocked Lionel.

Being the great friends that they were, her response surprised Dan less. He answered calmly, with measured foresight. "I do want to believe. I know we study science, but I'd love to see my family when I die. It's the ultimate fantasy, right?"

"Exactly!" Brodie shouted. "A fantasy."

Lionel chose that moment to strike. "It's been a hell of a lot of years, but this old man could use an ear or two. I'd like to share a story from my time in the army. And you guys seem like smart kids."

"We aren't kids, Sir," Danny began, but Brodie punched him again. This time, Danny punched her back, the pair suffering for their friendship with dead arms, as best friends do.

Lionel smiled, enjoying their rambunctiousness. It was the perfect time to start his crazy story. And so, he began. "My unit was involved in a science experiment of sorts. You ever hear of the Philadelphia experiment?"

Brodie's eyes widened and she gulped.

Danny stared. "That's a myth, isn't it?"

Lionel let out a chuckle. The suspense he'd built was amusing to him. He always started his story by mentioning the Philadelphia experiment for shock value. The implausible but widely believed story of a warship vanishing through physical manipulation and moving in time and space during a WWII experiment always got a rise out of people. Allegedly, the crew on board had been at best driven insane by the shift in time and space, and at worst had been fused into the body of the ship itself. Whether the experiment happened at all was none of Lionel's concern. "Well, I didn't take part in the Philadelphia experiment. But I was part of a team looking into life after death."

"Don't you have to die to look into that particular issue?" Danny asked, growing cockier the further down his beer he got.

"Well, naturally. And that's exactly what they did to my friend and crew member at the time, Bill Hunter."

"Wait, wait, wait," Brodie demanded, holding up her hand and gesturing for Stig to come over. "We all need another round for this story, I'm guessing."

Lionel smiled and winked, pleased to see that the girl had his full attention. Stig set beers in front of the trio and Lionel began to tell his story, a gleam of nostalgia in his eye.

Bill Hunter had been a peculiar man from the moment Lionel had met him. Large and gruff, with a raven crew cut and brown irises so dark they often looked black in the shadows, Bill was loud, confident, and lived his life without shame.

The first time Lionel had seen Bill, the man was lying on his bunk in his uniform, squeezing his dick through his pants as he bragged about his favourite evening pastime; a Wisconsin Blow Dryer. This, Lionel had soon discovered, was the act of ejaculating over a woman's face and proceeding to fart across the semen until it dried.

Bill was animatedly recounting how he had discovered a ready and willing participant at the brothel near the docks and had spent a long and expensive night jacking off and passing wind until the woman "looked to have aged sixty years overnight. No joke, she smiled up at me and her skin was pulled so tight I thought her eyes were gonna pop out of the sockets. Practically saw her brain back there."

Lionel had stood awkwardly in the room's doorway, unsure which bunk was his and already intimidated by the ragtag group of older participants in the experiment.

Bill had noticed him hovering there and grinned. "What's your pleasure?"

Flustered and mishearing, Lionel had responded by giving his own name.

"A Lionel? I've not heard of that one. What do you do to her? Or, more importantly, what does she do to you?"

When Lionel had bashfully admitted that this was his Christian name and not in fact something that could be requested as an extra at a whorehouse, the room had erupted into guffaws. From that moment, his nickname in the squad had been Sex Act, a name that Bill Hunter had delighted in bestowing on him.

As jovial as his first interaction with Bill had been, the pair soon sobered when they were partnered together on their intended mission. Both men had been selected due to their ability to endure extremes, but the pair were under no illusion that this experiment would be a walk in the park. Although it kept them off the front line, they were to be exposed to threats just as life-threatening as those who were left in the trenches.

Lionel had been an accomplished ice diver and knew

what it was like to feel death cresting in his internal organs and flummoxing his brain as he fought to reverse the effects of the crushing Arctic waters.

While Lionel thrived at freezing depths, Bill had traversed the highest mountains, forgoing oxygen for the power of his huge lungs and the stamina of his sheer, unwavering belligerence.

Together, they would attempt to fulfil the directives given in Project Scire, the allocated title being the Latin word for "know".

In retelling the story, as he had done just seven times during his long life, Lionel tended to skip over the preliminaries of the experiment. He didn't go into details about how he had felt when he had read the directive and watched it burn after reading. He mentioned that he and Bill had drawn straws to discover who would test the first prototype (Bill pulling the short straw), but he didn't explain the strange mixture of desolation and relief that had plagued him in the nights that followed. During the days, they were too distracted with the preparation to dwell on what it really meant to be a pawn in Project Scire. But at night, as is so often the case, the ceiling became the backdrop of a mind plagued by thoughts of mortality.

Outwardly, Bill had been overjoyed to draw the short straw, turning to Lionel and acting as though the chopped stick had been the intended goal all along. "Tough break, Sex Act. You get to watch me change history."

Two days before the experiment was due to launch, Lionel had woken from a fitful slumber to the sound of gentle whimpering. Bill was a huge lump, fully hidden underneath his covers, but the trembling that wracked his body shook the bedframe. He and Bill shared a room by that point, separated from the other participants unless they were using the bathroom and cafeteria. This was because the bulk of the experiment was to take place two-by-two, animals going into an ark that was destined to sink. Lionel had been relieved he was the only one to see Bill break down in that way, and he knew better than to give any inkling that he had been anything other than in a deep sleep when it happened.

Back to his exuberant self the next day, Bill greeted Lionel in the cafeteria with a mouth full of sausage. "Sex Act! Get enough beauty sleep, did ya?"

The other participants had chuckled, but the room was subdued. Many of the soldiers had tell-tale black rings under their eyes from troubled slumbers, and two had already disappeared from the programme. There was no explanation as to where they were, and Lionel knew better than to ask. Classified meant keep your mouth shut and focus on your job.

Bill's job was dying.

The objective was to "get answers" and return somehow from the point of death while retaining the knowledge that those with a pulse were not supposed to know.

The theory came from citizens who had come back from near-death experiences with a pervading sense that, at the point in which they moved into the afterlife, they were suddenly prescient to all the knowledge of the universe. Everything made sense to them and there were no longer any mysteries. From the contents at the farthest reaches of the cosmos to the reason why humans cry, speculation was arbitrary, and a deep certainty of all fact was a memory that lingered with many people who had been declared dead only to be drawn back into their bodies with a zap of a defibrillator or a timely tracheotomy that pumped air back into their withered lungs.

But omniscient cognition is not a state that can be sustained by the living. Each patient who reported they had experienced the phenomenon held rigid conviction that they had known the secrets of the universe in death but had forgotten them all upon being revived.

Some explained it as seeing multiple screens showing the universe in a flash. Others stated that they could think of a single question and immediately know the answer. This was naturally a skill that the military was desperate to obtain and weaponize.

If Bill failed, the method would be tweaked, and Lionel would take his turn at facing oblivion.

The morning of the first voyage into the afterlife, Bill cracked endless jokes and recounted his most vulgar stories, many of which included his favourite pastime. The worst involved a bad curry, a vigorous attempt at a Wisconsin Blow Dryer, and a poor girl getting more than just cum and farts in her face. If Lionel hadn't already felt queasy at the prospect of the mission, Bill's graphic story tipped him over the edge. He slipped out and puked in the multi-cubicle toilet block as quietly as he could.

By the time he returned to the lab, Bill was strapped flat against a gurney, sticky pads and catheters leading to endless wires and monitors. Even though he was about to be killed, Bill's heart rate was a steady 64, a fact that filled Lionel with admiration. He could feel his own heart hammering in his chest and hoped that, if he had to take up the mantel next, his BPM readings wouldn't show him up to be the coward he knew he was.

Colonel Thistles stood at the foot of Bill's bed, silently watching the medical crew as they worked. Thistles was a slender man with perma-tanned arms that were at odds with a face that appeared almost translucent it was so pale. The wrinkles around his eyes and on his forehead were deep and craggy, but a strong jaw and large teeth filling a mouth that barely ever moved meant that his lower face was practically baby-smooth. He was a man of contrasts, in both personality and appearance. Lionel had witnessed him quietly and coldly disciplining a soldier who had lost a boot on a trek due to not tying the laces properly. In the days after the telling-off, the soldier looked more harrowed than he ever had in battle, such was the terrifying power of Thistles' stern, quiet words gritted out through teeth that seldom parted.

But Lionel had also witnessed Thistles embracing a boy who had received the news that his parents and both sisters had been killed in a car accident back home. While the young man sobbed wracking yelps against the pips on Thistles' epaulettes, the commander had whispered gently into his ear, a tanned hand sliding up and down his back in slow circles until the cries had faded into numb resignation.

"Are you ready, Soldier?" Thistles asked Bill when the medics stepped back and stood respectfully with their hands over their groins as though they were trying to block a free kick.

"Send me to the stars!" Bill grinned.

"Remember, the objective is to retain the information you discover in the moments that you are legally dead. Understood?"

"I won't let you down." Bill's eyes hiked across to meet Lionel's, and he wiggled his eyebrows. It was an action an uncle would do to calm a child during a ruckus, and Lionel hated that he was the one being comforted at that moment.

He gave Bill a firm nod.

The doctor stepped forward and administered the medication. As the gold-tinged serum forced its way through the blood in Bill's vein, his heart rate suddenly jumped from 64 to 98. The toes of his left foot clenched within his sock, as though they were trying and failing to grip a pencil. His eyes rolled back, capillaries bursting and flooding the white orbs with red blotches. All visible skin puckered with goosebumps as the cooling agent went to work instantly preserving his flesh.

His heart monitor descended into a flatline.

"Start the clock," Thistles instructed.

A nurse whose only job appeared to be working the timer slammed gloved fingers against the stop clock button. Her eyes, the only features visible between a pale blue face mask and surgeon's cap, watched the racing numbers on the digital screen.

Just like that, Bill was dead.

Lionel wondered what he might possibly be experiencing in those minutes, each one endlessly long and torturously quick in turn. He just wanted it to be over. More than anything, he wanted it to work.

"Twelve minutes," the nurse with the stop clock told Thistles, eventually.

"Administer the reversal," Thistles said.

Lionel expected there to be a flurry of activity. Cries of "clear!" and the ringing fuzz of a defibrillator jerking electricity into declining chest muscle. But the doctor simply stepped forward and plunged a second serum into Bill's arm catheter. This one had a pearlescent green tinge to it and appeared to glitter under the white lights of the surgery.

Bill's skin bloomed with spreading pink as the chilling effects of the initial serum were reversed. His mouth opened and closed a few times, like a fish on land, and he rose up off the bed like the girl in *The Exorcist* when his lungs kicked back into action and scorching air inflated the drooping bags of stilled bronchi. It looked like agony, and Lionel couldn't help but stare at the floor until his friend had stopped gasping and slumped back on the gurney, somewhat revived.

Thistles crouched beside him. "Soldier, do you remember what you learned."

Bill's bloodshot eyes locked onto the commander. He nodded.

"Everybody out," Thistles barked, reaching for a pad and pencil.

As much as Lionel wanted to know what was said between the colonel and the man who had just been dead for twelve entire minutes, he figured he would find out when Bill returned to their dorm. But, three hours later, Bill stepped into the room with zombie-like fugue, his feet sliding along the floor.

Lionel sat on his bed, watching. "Are you okay, man?"

Bill glanced at him his expression bleary. "Tired," he mumbled, rolling onto his bunk.

Though desperate to ask questions, Lionel respected his teammate's need to rest and managed to keep his mouth shut to let him sleep. But every time Lionel looked over, Bill was wide awake, staring up at the ceiling with wide eyes that had the same haunted glaze as a soldier with shellshock.

The next morning, Lionel awoke to find Bill's face directly above his own, staring intently down at him. Gasping, Lionel flinched and scooched up the mattress, his pillows riding up behind his upper arms as he struggled to get Bill out of his personal space.

Bill placed his hands on Lionel's shoulders, pinning him, his nose now barely a centimetre away from Lionel's. The red blotches of the busted capillaries in the whites of his eyes looked like spatter from a gunshot strewn across white kitchen tiles.

"We aren't equipped," Bill hissed. "You'll see. You'll go next. But we've already gone too far."

Saliva spilt from Bill's lower lip and landed in the gully of Lionel's Cupid's bow. The warm wetness trickled slowly down and threatened to enter his mouth, the stench of coffee and tooth decay flooding his nostrils. He pressed his lips tighter, which only made him breathe more heavily through his nose.

Then Bill released him and stood straight, smiling a dazed little smile and humming a tune. "Breakfast time," the big man said, moving to the door.

"Bill, you're not wearing pants," Lionel blurted.

Looking down, Bill laughed at the sight of his dick swinging in the breeze. "Oh, that's right. We're supposed to be ashamed."

Lionel sat still as Bill laughed maniacally and went to

his drawer, tugging out a pair of grey sweatpants and clambering into them with the comically exaggerated movements of a clown in mime.

There was only one thing that Lionel had been certain of that moment. Something had gone terribly wrong.

His suspicions were confirmed tenfold over the following two days. It began with small things. He'd catch Bill observing the other soldiers with the bemused curiosity of a zoo visitor watching the apes. There was a kinship there, a deep knowledge that there were similarities at the very core of their species. But there was also a clear divide. A superiority.

The other men swerved to avoid him in the cafeteria. Gone was the centre of attention, his booming voice captivating the room with outlandish stories of bukkake and flatulence. In the place of the old Bill was a new Bill who experienced the world through different eyes. Eyes that had seen too much.

Lionel noticed something else in Bill, a cruelty that hadn't been there before. He would casually stride up behind one of the soldiers and whisper, a satisfied smile playing on his lips. The men would lurch away, immediately frightened of Bill's overbearing aura, and then the uttered phrase would sink in, and their faces would drift through puzzlement, anger, hurt, and resignation. It was like watching a man inflict the stages of grief onto a person with the power of a few words.

At night, Lionel lay awake, too frightened to let his guard down. He knew when Bill was watching him; could feel the disgust and animosity building. It seemed to Lionel that Bill had become the troubled child forced too early into adulthood, rampaging through the garden to try and find insects, a magnifying glass concealed in his pocket. After ripping off legs and wings, all that would be left was a motionless body to burn in the afternoon sun.

They were all just insects to him, now.

Including Bill himself.

The third night, when Bill slunk out of bed, Lionel felt his entire body stiffen in instinctive fear. But the big man moved straight to the door. Before it closed behind him, Lionel heard the distinctive squeak of the toilet block entrance being pushed open.

Alone in the room, he let himself relax for the precious minutes that Bill would be away. Sleep-deprived, he hadn't realised he'd drifted off until he awoke to distant shouts.

Immediately primed for battle, Lionel leapt from his bunk and raced out onto the corridor. A wall of stench stopped him in his tracks.

Soldiers taking part in the experiments stood outside the toilet block, most posed like comic vampires, their crooked elbows thrown across mouths and noses trying desperately to block the scent of shit that emanated from the cubicles. Down the hallway, a young soldier bent over his knees, puking, tears streaming down his face.

Lionel approached the bathroom.

A corporal, eyes wild, shook his head with frantic urgency, but Lionel ignored him. He needed to see his teammate.

Steeling himself by switching off the part of his brain that wanted him to run, Lionel slipped into the bathroom and found Bill sprawled on the tiles. A plastic bag coated in brown slicks of excrement lay empty at his side. All around him, Bill had smeared the crap, his hands covered, swirls daubing the tiled floor in neat circles like a skimmed plaster ceiling.

"That's you, Lionel!" Bill greeted him.

This was an impressive feat.

For one thing, there was no way Bill could smell him over the stench of sewage in the room.

For another, Bill's eyes were no longer in his face. They lay in the mess between Bill's legs, one popped and leaking fluid as it deflated, the other elegantly draped with its own optic nerve.

Though most of Bill's collected turds were spread across the floor, two had been wedged into his eye sockets and squashed flat.

He grinned up at Lionel as though he could see him perfectly through the two packed sockets. Spreading out his hands, gobbets of shit flying from his fingers and spattering the wall, he looked proud of what he'd achieved. "This is us. Humans," he declared.

"Bill," Lionel had said, forcing words through the saliva that filled his mouth and the constriction in his throat, "you need to stop."

"Stop? Why should I stop? There is nothing good once we die. I know everything. You'll come back and you'll spend the rest of your life removing the best people from this world. That's what this whole programme is. That's what people do, Lionel. They remove the best ones when they can because the worst ones allow the world to continue the way they want it to." Bill paused then, confused, his faeces-packed face tilting down at the smears he continued to make on the ground between his crossed legs. "We aren't the good ones, Lionel. We're the devils in charge."

Thistles burst through the door, soldiers in masks at his sides. They hauled Bill to his feet and dragged him out of the communal bathroom, which had always seemed sterile and cold but somehow felt uncharacteristically full of life because of the smeared swirls of shit on the floor.

Three nights later, Lionel stood in the toilet block brushing his teeth. The army had brought in a cleaning team who had managed to sluice every last speck of Bill's shit off the walls and floor. Lionel was due to try the tweaked experimental serum the next day, and he was afraid. Experiencing a sudden cramp, he left the toothbrush on the sink and ducked into a stall. If he hadn't moved fast, he could have left a similar sight to the one Bill had deposited for the cleaners.

Afterwards, he heard someone screaming down the hall. It wasn't Bill, but it was about him.

Granger, a tough, tall soldier who had taken one form of the serum that day (he'd previously fought in three battles on the frontline and miraculously come out unscathed), was yelling. "I see Bill! He's following me. Don't you see him? He's in my room again!"

When Lionel walked past Granger's dorm the next day, flanked by the nurses, there was no sign of the man. His bunk had been stripped, the mattress rolled and placed at the foot of the bed.

Lionel was more afraid of gouging out his own eyes and packing them with shit than he was of being induced into a state of death. Even so, as he lay back on the gurney and watched the pearlescent fluid entering his arm, he felt unbridled fear at the thought of learning the world's secrets. Some things, the ones that in the past he may have found most thrilling, he didn't want to know anymore. He kept his eyes on his BPM and tried to keep it a steady 76. Just before he died, the numbers spiked, but by then he didn't care.

He woke to find Thistles sitting beside him, the man's slender fingers folded around a crossed knee.

Then the questions began.

"So, you learned all the secrets of the world?" Brodie gawped.

A visible expression of disbelief on his face, Danny nudged her. "Come on. This story is a hundred layers of bullshit."

"Bill shit," Brodie corrected with a sly smile that Lionel returned.

Damn, he liked this kid. She was witty and smart and if Lionel had ever been able to have a family, he would have hoped his daughter was a lot like her.

"So, what does someone do with all that information? You'd think the army would have tasked you with some pretty serious secret missions over the years." Danny was beginning to look bored and a little drunk.

"Oh, they did. They surely did," Lionel said, never taking his eyes from Brodie.

"You could use someone like him on your programme," Dan told her before glancing back to Lionel. "Brodie's some kind of medical genius. She's going to change the world. Make everyone live longer."

"She certainly would have," Lionel agreed, softly.

He watched realisation dawn in Brodie a second before he plunged his blade into her throat. She truly was a smart cookie, for such a young kid. The knife he kept concealed in his fist split her jugular, a wound that would give her all the answers, too, in just a few seconds. She gasped, her throat emitting a gargling squeak as blood pumped around the blade, drowning her lungs. Brodie limply raised her arm and cupped her fingers around Lionel's hand, blood loss already weakening her limbs and fogging the instructions sent from brain to muscles.

Danny recoiled at the spray of crimson that pumped from his friend's neck. He stumbled away from his bar stool as Lionel ripped the blade away, letting Brodie's head slam down into the puddle of blood on the bar. Her body folded, her face and hair sliding through the blood and beer as she tipped backwards off her own stool and landed on the floor.

"What are you doing?" Danny screeched. His hands flapped around, an urge to help his friend being overridden by his brain's need to keep him at a relatively safe distance from the knife. "She was brilliant. She was going to save countless lives, you idiot!"

Lionel sighed, standing and making his way to the door. Oh, he knew that alright. Brodie would have elongated people's lives by a good 70 years at least. He saw it, back in 1958. He'd known it all along.

Just like he'd known that Albert Moore could change the world back in 1962. Then there was Jenny Alvarez in 1977. Five others after that. Young, eager faces, who had listened to his story with interest and flinched away seconds before his knife hit, knowing what was coming.

Lionel stepped out into the lashing rain and strode determinedly past the car waiting for him in the car park. Someone could have shouted his name, or maybe it was just a distant car horn distorted in the rain. He quickened his steps, heading out onto the empty highway. He crossed and stood on the bridge footpath, staring at the water rushing below. He wasn't sure why he always told them his story. There was something in that moment where they worked out why he was there that made him feel connected to them. It was some kind of twisted absolution and he wondered if it would have been better for Brodie if he'd simply stabbed her the moment she entered the bar.

He gripped the railing and was about to climb when a hand landed flat on his shoulder.

"Don't do it, soldier."

"It's enough. We've done enough."

"Just two more, Sex Act. Just two more. We'll be in touch." The facilitator walked away, the puddles swallowing the sound of his footsteps.

Through the sluicing rain, Bill Hunter's ice-white hands gripped the outer railings of the bridge and he stared back at Lionel with his eyes still packed with shit. Bill's spectre had followed Lionel ever since he came back.

In the way that Granger had been driven mad by the ghostly presence in his dorm room from the moment Bill was euthanised, Lionel had seen Bill's blank sockets staring back at him in every mirror and every shop window. He entered his apartment each night to the faint stench of shit and felt the couch depress slightly when Bill joined him as he drank whiskey and watched mind-numbing TV to fall asleep. If he turned fast enough he could see the man sitting beside him. Bill, who loved disgusting stories of depravity, did not deserve the eternal hell that knowing all had brought him.

Although Lionel had considered ending it all on numerous occasions while washing the blood of bright young teens from his hands, the eyeless man who stood behind him in the bathroom mirror each time was a constant reminder that there would be no peace in death for him. He could do nothing but comply with his orders because the ones who had been to the other side Bill clung to like wasps around a summer cider. And that would be his fate, too.

Just two more.

If only it were true.

Striding away from the bridge, Lionel found the nearest budget motel and stripped his clothes, letting them fall to the floor in a sodden heap. He clambered between the scratchy sheets and smelled cigarette smoke and the musty sourness of another man's nape on his pillow.

The bed rocked when Bill clambered in beside him.

Bill's spectre was always more solid just after an assassination. As though he was drawn to the completed mission—a spiritual purpose he just couldn't shake in death.

Lionel rolled over and came face to face with him and wanted to cry for Brodie, for Bill, and for himself. "You know what, Bill? The saddest thing I learned from the other side is that nothing is random. Is that what made you so crazy?"

The expressionless brown sockets stared back. Peering into those sightless eyes packed full of human waste, Lionel knew that there was one undeniably bleak and terrible truth that he had learned on the other side: the truth about freedom.

It was rigged.

About the Author

MJ Mars is a geek, ghoul, and horror enthusiast living in Lancaster, UK. Her debut novel, *The Suffering*, was published by Wicked House in 2023. When she isn't writing, you'll find MJ playing pool, trying to skateboard (badly), or listening to rock music. She owes every success to her mis-spent youth.

Acknowledgements

I have overwhelming gratitude toward my new friends in the book world, without whom I wouldn't be living my best life.

Patrick Reuman at Wicked House, thank you for taking a shot on *The Suffering* and making all my dreams come true. With additional thanks to the incredible authors, my WH brothers and sisters, who have shared their knowledge and cheered me on every step of the way: Andrew Najberg, Blaine Daigle, Duncan Ralston, David Blair, Will Gray, Jon Cohn, Josh Hill, Jeremy Eads, Caleb Jones, Cassandra O'Sullivan Sachar, Westley Smith, Axl Malton, Bryan Alaspa, Nick McAnulty, Joe Scipione, Elizabeth Devecchi, Brad Ricks, and the whole team at Wicked House. This is a rapidly growing family and I love and appreciate every one of you!

In the UK, I'd like to give a huge shout out to The Sassy Squad, Leigh Kenny and Sarah Jules, who have spent countless hours making me laugh, listening to me moan, and generally keeping me sane during this crazy year. Additional thanks to 'Mum and Dad', Elizabeth J. Brown and M. L. Rayner, whose wisdom in the field of self-publishing is unsurpassed, and the rest of the UK Authors group (with an extra shout-out to Sharron Joy Reads who is the most wonderful human) for always being there. Can't wait to meet you all for obligatory tea and biscuits.

I owe Christy Aldridge at Grim Poppy Design a drink for reaching into my head and pulling out my dream book cover. As I said to you at the time, I want to wallpaper my house with it! You're amazing.

Special thanks to Tiffany Koplin, whose casual suggestions, ("Hey, have you thought about signing up to Authorcon?" "Why don't you release a chapbook ready for Books and Brews?" etc) have pushed me out of my comfort zone, blasted my imposter syndrome out of the water, and allowed me to achieve so many things in the last year I can't believe it's actually happened. Aside from everything you do for us authors in the Books of Horror Group, I can personally say that I wouldn't have been to the US, wouldn't have been on stage with Penn and Teller, wouldn't have met my literary hero, Paul Tremblay, and wouldn't be writing this dedication in my own short story collection right now. You're a queen and Goddess, and we love you.

Speaking of Books of Horror, thank you to every reader, reviewer, encouraging commenter, and author who takes part in the group and spreads love in a weary world.

And last but not least, thank you to Jamie. The best tech support, chauffeur, logistics manager, drinking buddy, ideas guy, gig pal, skate and bass tutor, hype-man, and hubby a gal could ever have.

Trigger Warnings

General:
Gore, viscera, excrement, puke, family issues, aliens, monsters.

Personal:
British spellings.

If you don't like representations of diverse sexual identity, you'll probably have an issue with *Fallen Eagles and Aces*/my work in general. The horror community is a safe space - we like it queer around here.